Ransom's Mountain

Paul Wheelahan

A Black Horse Western

ROBERT HALE · LONDON

ISBN 0 7090 7401 8

Robert Hale Limited
Clerkenwell House
Clerkenwell Green
London EC1R 0HT

Typeset by
Derek Doyle & Associates, Liverpool.
Printed and bound in Great Britain by
Antony Rowe Limited, Wiltshire

ONE

HALF-WAY TO HEAVEN

They were hanging Barney Hackett by the pearly light of dawn.

From his cell above the courthouse Buck Conway watched the spectacle in frozen stillness, wide-eyed and unblinking. No quick quips or ready smile now from the dashing badman in this grisly hour of retribution as the body of his former cell-mate jerked and threshed on the fraying end of that yellow rope, his head six feet below the crossbeam and boot-heels a bare but oh so vital six inches above the hard-packed sand of the yard.

'God Amighty!' he choked out. 'How long does it take to kill a loser anyway?'

The answer to that was . . . far longer than most folks thought.

Although he mightn't look the part at that

moment, Conway was widely regarded around Plainsville as the most exciting and newsworthy prisoner to grace the marshals' jailhouse in years, a man who could make light of almost anything, even the official charge under which he'd been arrested, namely the cold-blooded backshooting murder of two citizens over in Stageville.

But where even steel bars or grave accusations lodged before a granite-faced judge had failed to curb the prisoner's quick tongue, the sight of that now limp figure swaying on the gibbet surrounded by a select circle of somber-faced witnesses – all glad to see him put to death like a dog – had succeeded only too well.

The authorities had vowed to try, convict and hang Hackett, and they'd done it. Worse still, Marshals Bourke and Needham had vowed to dispatch Conway, the accused killer, in exactly the same way, yet he'd never really believed them until that moment.

So it was that upon returning from their execution, the renowned two-man team of manhunting marshals were astonished to find their hitherto cockiest-ever prisoner now huddled in terror in a cold cell corner, clutching at the bars. Neither man could conceal his satisfaction in seeing such a man finally cut down to size by the full realization of just how desperate his situation really was.

'One down and one to go, Conway.' There was no compassion in Needham's make-up. Not for this breed. 'Better make your peace, killer, for as sure as God made little green apples, where

Hackett is right now is where you'll be inside the week. Our case against you is watertight, scum.'

The face of the huddled figure was blotted out by the loose fall of his long hair as Conway hung his head. It was his worse moment since his arrest. He hated them for seeing him like this, but hated himself even worse for exposing the pallid under-belly of his fear.

Yet even in his moment of terror the prisoner managed to muster enough defiance to whisper through chattering teeth, 'Not without a witness it ain't no way watertight.'

He tried desperately to back this up with a mocking smile, but fear-frozen features wouldn't respond. He had to be content with watching some of the arrogance and assurance fade from his jailers' hard faces, telling him his taunt had hit home hard. For although the lawmen had produced two bullet-riddled corpses as evidence of murder most foul, and knew beyond doubt that Conway had gunned the Stageville pair down, their case against him remained entirely circumstantial. Without their eye witness, the case of the People *v.* Buck Conway might never come to trial.

It was ten miles as the crow flies from the county seat of Plainsville on the High Plains to Tracktown where the Whitefoot River came down out of the mountains. It was much closer to fifty if you made the journey by coach, horseback, riverboat or old-fashioned bootleather.

But ten miles or fifty might have easily seemed a

thousand when you considered the yawning difference between respectable, law-abiding Plainsville
and the brawling, boozing Whitefoot levee town
where summer saw the wild men return from long
months in the mountains with big money in their
Levis and a roaring thirst for 'civilization.'

The statuesque redheaded dancer from the Big
Dipper saloon might only be newcome to town, yet
she knew exactly what the wild boys were looking
for. Her. She was the long-legged, high-breasted
ideal of men who liked their whiskey straight and
their steaks thick, and knew it. So it came as something of a shock for her to realize that a man who
was surely the most impressive specimen her
hungry eyes had clapped on since the thaw, seemed
more interested in his glass and the barkeep's
boring conversation than in gorgeous, sexy her.

Lulu could never resist a challenge. She
sashayed right up to the tall, dark and broad-
shouldered stranger and, leaning back against the
bar to show off her lush figure to full advantage,
batted her eyelashes and waited for his response.

And waited.

Jack Ransom was well aware of the woman yet
his expression did not change. He knew where she
was coming from; a man would need to be both
blind and dumb not to. And he liked what he saw.
At the end of six months' trapping and hunting in
the rugged Heritage Range section of this sweep of
the Rockies, what Lulu was displaying so flamboyantly was what every red-blooded mountain man
had been dreaming of every single day of those

twenty-four weeks of freezing mornings, week-long hunts, Indian fights, avalanches and frostbite.

Ransom rated himself about as red-blooded as the next man. Yet he still wasn't buying.

When the Big Dipper's main attraction belatedly realized this, her reaction was swift and predictable.

'Well, pardon me all to hell!' she said loudly, straightening and swishing a diaphanous red scarf over one creamy shoulder as she raked him up and down with snapping eyes. 'I must be slipping. Seems I could always tell a colt from a gelding in the old days.'

This drew a ripple of mirth which quickly subsided. For while long-legged Lulu was newcome to Tracktown, Ransom and his partners had been summering along the Whitefoot for a full three seasons now. Long enough for the locals to know that sniggering at this Heritage Range fur-hunter or his friends wasn't the most prudent way to fill your lay-off time along the river.

Ransom sighed. He didn't want to wrangle with anybody today. This was rest-up time. Most men relaxed naturally but he had to work at it, being the kind of man he was: stern and uncompromising, never really one of the boys, a man in fact regarded by many as driven, aloof and remote. And he could be hard. Real hard.

He managed a smile, aware they were attracting attention. He produced a bill and placed it on the bar.

'Give the lady whatever she wants, Rick.' He dropped her a wink. 'Another time, maybe?'

Only a saloon chippy with a real high opinion of herself and a tetchy disposition to go with it would react the way she did.

'Keep your money, loser,' she said loudly, feeding on the mob's attention. 'You might use it to buy yourself a good hot-water bottle to cuddle up with tonight. That is your sleepin' choice, I take it.'

He paused at her taunt, then kept going as a familiar voice sounded from over by the piano.

'Better go easy, gal!' it advised. There was no mistaking the husky outdoor tones of his partner Dusty Hush. 'Shouldn't fuss with a hard-nosed winner like Jack, not if you value your ass.'

'Winner?' She snorted, mad clear through now. Her angry eyes cut across to where Ransom's grinning Heritage Range partners, Hush and Cassidy, were adding to their evergrowing collection of empty beer-pots atop the piano. 'Him? You must be joking.'

'No joke, gal,' assured big Cassidy. 'Ask anybody. Why, we even call him Jack the Winner in these parts. Ain't that so, boys?'

Heads nodded and Ransom, pausing with hands atop the slatted doors, winced a little. That 'Jack the Winner' tag just wouldn't leave him, even though it was over two years now since he'd won that booze-fuelled, hundred-mile, dog-sled race across the Rockies from Utah, in the process surviving an attack by a grizzly and being forced to swim the icy Medicine Bend rapids to escape.

He waited. He didn't have to wait long.

'What's he win at?' Lulu bawled, playing to the gallery. 'Solitaire?'

The crack might have been vaguely amusing, yet Ransom's expression was taut as he made his way south along Main. He was not an easy-smiling man nor even an overly sociable one most times. Yet that was just the way he was, maybe how he would always be now, or so he found himself brooding. For he would turn thirty-five on November 6 next. Half-way to heaven – if that was where he was headed – he sensed the pattern of his life was settling into routine. He trapped all winter and hunted through till spring. In the brief summer months, in the shadows of the mighty mountains, he read, dreamed and fished the green waters of the Whitefoot. And just like all of his breed, went searching for love and excitement anyplace they might be found.

Finding excitement presented no problem. Down along the Whitefoot, in any one of a dozen ferry stops, forts, trading posts or those ramshackle collections of buildings masquerading as towns, a man could find his fill of gambling, brawling, boozing and whoring, pastimes which could and frequently did lead to the flash of naked blades beneath swinging saloon-lamps or gun duels fought to the death on open streets. It was a way of living that could lead to tears, regrets, scars, remorse, yes, and even sometimes to a kind of maturity and wisdom.

But love? That was something else again.

There just might be more females to the square

mile along Whitefoot River's meandering course
than anyplace in Wyoming, and most were available – at a price. Most successful fur-and-hide men
such as Ransom could easily afford that price. A
few lucky ones even got to find true love with
Jessie, Janet or Jane. Yet he had too much vanity
and pride to run with whores, along with a powerful conviction that if a man kept looking for love in
all the wrong places he might well miss out on his
chance at the real thing when and if it happened
by.

When and if. . . .

In his younger years, he'd mostly thought in
terms of 'when'. Now, cruising towards the half-way
point of his life the focus had shifted to 'if'.
Sometimes it felt like he'd forgotten how to
dream.

He sighed as he waited for an approaching
wagon to churn by before crossing the street.
Seemed he was moulded by nature to excel at this
life he led even if it seemed to bring him fewer and
fewer rewards of the kind that really counted.

Anyone seeing Ransom on the streets of this
wild town that day would be hard put to believe
this was a man confronting some kind of crisis in
his life. So powerfully made, so self-assured, he
appeared to personify the archetypal buckskinned
Westerner from head to toe.

But at that particular moment the mountain
man was acutely conscious of a sense of aloneness,
an ebbing of the forces that drove him. It was a
strange sort of solitary sadness that was rammed

home with brutal abruptness when he chanced to glance up at the wagon to see the little family seated on the high seat.

He stood staring after the mother, father and child seated together on the rough plank seat. They appeared dog-tired and looked beat as they rumbled by, yet they were together and looked as though they belonged that way. As he was never close with anyone. Not really.

He was a successful man. Yet that slack-jawed wagoner with the ass out of his chinos had what Jack Ransom had never had and didn't even know where to start looking for it.

'Shift your ass or git run under, peckerhead!'

The voice came right off the head of a banjo. Turning his head, he saw the rickety rig bearing down on him with three hostile faces scowling down as though they hoped he would stand his ground so that they might indeed run him down.

Ransom backed up and the rig churned on by, the mustached driver spraying a stream of tobacco juice messily over a creaking wheel.

He blinked in surprise. Had he really given ground that way? He shook his head. He must be one sick mountain man to get to fretting over next to nothing, then pass up a chance to teach some newcomers something about Whitefoot River manners.

He forced a mood change in the moments it took to complete his crossing. He sprang lightly up on to the high plankwalk and filled his deep chest with air as pure as sunlight. Enough soul-

13

searching and day-dreaming, Ransom, he warned himself severely. Then aloud, startling a passer by: 'All you're really searching for is chow, pilgrim!' He headed directly for the Squat and Gobble on the corner. Supper comprised a slab of juicy buffalo steak with tinned tomatoes, corn fries, pone bread and a sauce he was unable to identify, the lot washed down with three cracked crockery cups of whiskey aged in the oak for three whole days.

'Why, howdy there, Yankee boy.'

The Kentucky jug drawl was familiar, as were the faces as he slowly turned. Three of them. A rangy man around fifty in black hat, string tie and yellow vest flanked by two gaunt rannies in their twenties. Hardcases. Unshaven and hairy. If they weren't all Southerners then he wouldn't recognize a Secesh if he found one in his skivvies. He'd sighted them once before today, on the street in the trap. Only thing that had changed since seemed to be their attitude. The cornpone trio now seemed to be trying to appear friendly but it didn't sit well on any of them. Although grimed and travel-stained, they didn't appear short of a dollar. Plenty artillery, he observed.

He let a held breath go. He'd achieved some kind of calm following his uncharacteristic attack of introspection on Main Street, didn't want to risk it slipping away on him now.

'What?' His tone was brusque. He might feel at peace, but he sure didn't need company.

14

The older man surveyed him through washed out eyes.

'Uh, huh, guess you're the one ah'm a-lookin' for, sure 'nuff.'

'Guess again, pops. I don't know you.'

His tone was harsh, his manner dismissive. But the Southerner was unfazed. His name was Smith, he advised, and he and his sons were in the market for a mountain guide. The best there was. Wanted someone to take them all the way up to Ghost Mountain west of the divide. Searching for kin, so he claimed.

Ransom frowned, vaguely interested despite himself. Ghost Mountain was remote and inhospitable but with plenty pretty country 'twixt here and there. There'd been camp-fire rumors aplenty of strange activities up in that region in recent times. He didn't necessarily believe the stories, yet he felt a vague stir of curiosity, which he quickly suppressed.

'You've got the wrong party,' he grunted. 'I'm a fur man, not a trail scout.'

He broke off as Smith senior produced a wad of banknotes. It was thick as a wrestler's neck.

'How much to escort us folks up to Ghost Mountain, Mister Ransom, suh?'

The Southerner was confident, plainly convinced money would unlock all doors, but for some reason Ransom was only irritated now.

'You've used up your dallying time,' he stated flatly. 'Go bother someone else.'

To his surprise the younger and leaner of the

sons appeared to take offence. Ransom promptly drew himself to full height, intent on intimidating the fellow with his dimensions. Yet the kid still looked snaky, and belatedly Ransom realized where his courage was coming from. The cracker wore a gunbelt beneath a faded old Confederate jacket, and had his bony right hand wrapped round the handle of a Colt .44.

Why, the miserable little shit! A man could snap him in two!

'All right, 'nuff of that fool stuff, boy,' the father twanged, elbowing the son to one side. The faded eyes snapped at Ransom. The man was peeved, yet plainly more disappointed than anything. 'You're a mean son of a bitch, mountain man, but then ah cain't say ah wasn't warned 'bout that. But the offer's still open iffen you change your mind.'

At that point Ransom might well have asked just what could possibly be important enough for any man to want to outlay a big parcel of cash to undertake that punishing journey up to Ghost Mountain in the summertime.

But he didn't. Simply wasn't interested enough. He turned his back to order another aged-by-the-hour sourmash, and when he looked again, the trio was noplace to be seen.

He downed three more drinks and was ordering what he intended to be his last, when romance of a kind again intruded on this odd day he was having.

A group comprising a fat lady, three prospectors, a black trooper and a portly gentleman in a frock-coat had been taking on freight heavily nearby and growing increasingly noisy as a result, ever since his arrival.

Suddenly the fat lady hollered, 'Why you sneaky-handed jackanape, I'll teach you to keep hands to yourself!' She hauled off and slammed the big man with her pocket-book.

The man lashed back instinctively and knocked the woman on her backside. The husky trooper punched the miner behind his left ear to send him reeling back against the bar, eyes rolling in their sockets. The second miner deliberately set his glass aside and kicked the trooper in the groin. The trooper doubled over and staggered into the third prospector, who brought a swinging chair crashing down on his bent back. Going down, the trooper lashed out with a kick and collected the gent in the frock-coat, knocking him backwards and upsetting a whole row of tables. In the excitement, someone trod on the woman who began screaming like it was vampire night in Transylvania and all the windows were open.

Everybody started fighting.

Disgust high in his throat, Ransom scooped up his hat and left them to it, making his way out on to the front porch. He was adjusting his hat to the right angle in the velvet twilight when a by now unwelcomely familiar voice sounded close by:

'Y'all changed your mind, cousin? Offer still holds. Two hundred dollars down, another three when you git us all up on thet old man mountain.'

Jack Ransom was irritated to confront the

Southerners again, with Smith senior holding up his fistful of dollars like it was carrots and he was the donkey. At first, that was. But in the space of mere moments, with the Squat and Gobble rocking to the beat of a rafter-rattling brawl, and the strangely unsettling day he'd just put in all too fresh in his mind, suddenly the 'attractions' of Tracktown seemed to vanish in comparison with the prospect of maybe a week or so up in the pristine high country, away from it all and hopefully away from his private demons.

'Five hundred now and five more when we reach the foot of the Ghost,' he countered, and Daddy Smith almost grinned. He would have gone higher.

So it was that in the summertime in the year of the Lord, 1873, 'Jack the Winner' Ransom turned his back on the fleshpots of the flatlands and returned to the mountains he'd so eagerly quit just six short weeks earlier. He was taking on the sort of work he despised in the hire of men he neither liked nor trusted, was headed for a sector of the mountains rumored to to be building up to some kind of big trouble.

The question was why he was going, and not even he knew the answer to that. Not clearly, anyway. All he knew was that it felt good to be alone in the mountains again – for such was his contempt of his clients that this was how he regarded himself. Alone and trouble free.

His only twinge of guilt centered on the fact that, so eager was he to quit Tracktown, he hadn't even taken the time to inform Cassidy and Hush of his plans.

The guilt dispersed as he realized he wouldn't miss them one bit. Yet this realization brought a frown. Maybe 'Jack the Winner' was looking to wind up as 'Jack the Hermit' one day soon, the solitary way he was heading in life.

He grinned as Blue, his sure-footed half-quarter and half-Morgan horse carried him up and over a grassy hummock to bring yet another green-and-gold mountain vista into view. 'This is what you wanted, pilgrim,' he told himself out loud. 'So don't go taking any of it too serious; just relax and enjoy the ride.'

Which was exactly what he did. It was easy enough to do up here, even for him. For it was true what the old-time mountain men liked to brag: 'If the Rockies in summertime don't do it for you, then you're done for.'

TWO

RIMROCK RIDERS

Sunlight sparkled across the high valley.

'Nary a sign, girl.'

The gray-bearded man snapped his brass tele-scope shut and rested one elbow on the look-out rock supporting his sturdy body. To his left was the young woman and the valley, to the right the vast and tumbledown sweep of rolling hills leading west in the direction of hidden Glacier Canyon and the remote and white crested crown of Ghost Mountain.

'What did you expect to see, Harry?'

He shrugged.

'Something ... anything, I guess....' Harry Duval screwed up his eyes as again he cut his gaze westwards. Out there below the upthrusting peaks of the Rockies lay a tumbled mountainscape of valley, canyon, precipice, rimrock and basin which even the hardiest of mountain men visited but rarely, and which in summertime could reasonably be expected to show little sign of human intrusion, even by the Shoshone. Yet he was convinced he'd glimpsed movement far off in the direction of the Ghost along Squaw Trail just the previous night. Again. As a consequence he'd been out here since first light, panning the terrain with his captain's telescope but without glimpsing anything on two legs but one grouchy brown grizzly hunting honey.

For many reasons, it was vital that Harry Duval should know if there were intruders anyplace near Eliza Valley. Imperative.

'I'm not afraid,' Laura said in her quiet way. 'Why should you be?'

She wasn't criticizing, just commenting. Criticism wasn't in her make-up. Sometimes she seemed without frailty, fault or weaknesses in the eyes of her companion, and this confounded him. For Harry Duval, although basically a decent man despite the shadow of an unsavory past, reckoned he had enough weaknesses in his make-up for a dozen. Hence he could only marvel at someone with virtue and character to burn.

'We should be getting back, girl,' he grunted finally. 'Light'll shortly be beginning to go. Don't want you catching chill.'

She smiled at him, the wind tumbling dark wavy hair about her face.

'You really do look out for me, don't you, Harry?'

'That's what I'm being paid for.'

'No, it's more than that. You really care for

people, and that's sweet, although I must say I find it a little puzzling.'

He let that pass, sensed she was alluding to his background, some of which she was familiar with, although luckily not all. They started off together, the man toying with his telescope, the woman drinking in the kind of landscape Plains folk never got to see.

The waning afternoon sun cast the long shadows of majestic pines and firs far across the valley floor, and the strengthening murmur of the wind in the topmost branches was bringing a chill down off the snow. Sunken and protected by windbreaks of mighty trees, the valley was snugly set away up here above Skyline Plateau, yet there was no avoiding the cold even in summer. Early trappers had erected a stout cabin in Eliza Valley before realizing that the real hunting lands lay two days southwest in the Heritage Range region. The dwelling had remained isolated and rarely visited until this odd couple from the High Plains had arrived recently to fix it up and move in.

'You understand why you puzzle me, don't you, Harry?'

'Huh?' His thoughts were elsewhere. Safety and security dominated Duval's days up here. There was every good reason why this should be so. He added grudgingly, 'OK, just why is that, girl?'

'Why, because you've turned out to be a gentle and caring man, of course. Someone I can trust.'

Mostly they didn't talk overmuch. It was a peaceful, easy silence between two people thrown together by circumstance. She was a devout Quaker who spent a deal of time praying and such-like. For his part, Harry Duval filled his days studying the bird-life, keeping his own counsel, and staying sharp. Real sharp.

He tugged at the short white whiskers that framed his nut-brown face.

'I don't much care to dwell on my past, if that's what you're hinting at, Laura.'

'Are you ashamed of it?'

'You know, it ain't like you to bother a body about things like that.'

'Oh, I don't want to bother you, Harry . . . and of course I won't mention it again. It's really none of my business.'

He studied her profile as they approached a clump of heavy cedars which stood like so many aging and dignified men gathered together for an evening yarn before night took over.

Shady Harry considered Laura Conway as about the finest stamp of young womanhood he'd ever encountered. He'd been taken by her beauty first up but had come to admire her character and strength even more since their arrival in the valley.

'It's all right, girl. Reckon I understand you being curious about me and howcome I'm tied in with your husband some. You'd like to know more about me so you can better see what kind of light that throws on Buck, him and me being friends and all. Ain't that the truth of it?'

Laura halted, facing him. He saw his words strike home, saw the hurt there.

'Buck's not a real badman, is he, Harry? I know what they say . . . and what he did . . . but surely that doesn't mean. . . .'

He reached out and touched her hand, an aging fading rogue with a past and a heart.

'Your Buck's OK, honey,' he assured, wishing he believed it. He was saved from saying more as the cedars shook before a violent gust and the cold wind hit them, feathering Duval's wiry whiskers and pressing Laura's plain gray dress against the graceful outlines of her body. He nodded. 'Better hasten. The chill, you know.'

'We both know it doesn't matter at all what I might catch or come down with, Harry,' she said in that sober way she had sometimes. They hurried through the surging green surf of the long grass. 'Indeed, I suppose I should really welcome catching some disease. A fatal one, even.'

He hated it whenever she spoke this way even though well aware of the reason for it.

Laura Conway understood her companion's feelings in this regard. After all, she was just twenty-three years of age, seemingly with her whole life ahead of her, wedded to a man she loved. She enjoyed perfect health and vitality, yet had little if any expectation of leaving this valley alive, of ever getting to celebrate her twenty-fourth birthday.

But acceptance of something inevitable and actually welcoming it could be two markedly different matters.

In her heart, she'd almost come to terms with

what she regarded as her fate, yet it was never going to be easy to surrender her young life and all her joy in it when and if it should come time for her to do so.

To her way of thinking, death should have no place in this wonderful setting. And yet she felt it all about her as they followed an animal pad up a gentle gradient which accessed a wider view of the west, where the sun was falling swiftly over the cedars, daubing in gold both the rock steeple of Hightower along with the granite outcrop and the white pine that marked the course of distant Squaw Trail, which linked Ghost Mountain and Glacier Canyon with Skyline Plateau and the foothills below.

Death was in the wind, in the turbulent tossing of the horizon trees and the whispering rustle of the grasses about her skirt. The sudden sharp hoot of an owl coming from the direction of the cabin sounded eerie and caused the young woman to shiver. Her end was as inevitable as the sunset, she knew. For by poison, blade, fire or by falling, the time would come when Laura Conway must take her own young life.

Judson Smith said, 'Why we stoppin', Yankee?'

'Simple,' Ransom replied, reining in and swinging down. 'This is as far as I go.'

The clansmen stared around. The last climbing ten miles of Squaw Trail had boosted them high and to the north-west of Skyline Plateau across increasingly roughening country to this ugly slab-stoned ridge with a bulking overhang of cedars to their right, a steep slope of granitic outcropping to their left and an inviting sweep of tolerably open landscape stretching away in the direction the trail was heading, north-west.

The wind blew like a bitch and they clutched at their hats whenever it gusted. Ransom sat Blue some distance apart from the others, his back to the granite outcroppings. He wasn't cast-iron certain there would be trouble, but if it came he wouldn't be surprised.

Nor would he avoid it.

He'd had a bellyful of Smiths.

He had to concede that this came as no surprise. A man would customarily only take on a hitch like this when hard up for money, felt good about his clients or maybe just wanted to do somebody a good turn.

None of these criteria applied to his signing up with the redneck Southerner and his ugly sons.

It had been an unwise move from the outset. He wasn't short of money and had disliked his hirers on sight, yet had grabbed up their offer anyway. Those had been the wrong set of circumstances under which to undertake a long and testing trek and he was aware of that fact well before reaching this point in the journey.

Daddy Smith and his offspring were scum.

They were bad campers and lousy trailsmen. They bitched endlessly, bucked his authority every inch, were clannish, secretive, quick-tempered, ornery – and almost certainly were owlhoot.

It was this last suspicion, hardened by little things he'd seen, sensed and felt more and more strongly over the past twenty-four hours, backed up by a crawling hunch that his clients might be fixing to try some sneak play, which had caused him to make up his mind fast. Trail's end for this outfit was right here in this patch of granite country. They'd come to the parting of the ways.

His clients didn't see it that way.

Daddy Smith's saddle leather creaked ominously as he shifted position to stare at his sons. He then peered north-west before spitting a long stream of brown tobacco-juice between his horse's ears.

'Guess y'all's under a misapprehension, Yankee boy. You hired to take us to the Ghost, and if ah ain't mistook that's it far yonder on the horizon.'

'Right,' Ransom replied. 'That's it, in full sight. Nothing but open and empty country 'twixt here and there, so you don't need me any longer.'

Another silence.

Ransom read the quietness and didn't like it. The Smiths would argue with you simply because you set up camp one side of the trail when they favored the other. The fact that they weren't yet objecting violently to his abrupt declaration suggested they were preoccupied with something else. Their slow reaction was out of character.

Some psychic signal seemed to pass between the horsemen, and suddenly they were fanning out, making space between one another and easing their trail-weary horses towards him, almost as if they had rehearsed.

It struck Jack Ransom that this might well be the case.

The bastards!

'Seems to me when a feller makes a contract he oughta stick by it, Daddy,' remarked the white-shirted elder son, hitching at his greasy shell belt.

'And not abandon trustin' citizens to the dangers of the wild,' his denim-garbed brother affirmed. 'Of course, we all are talkin' down-home custom, ain't we. What white men'll do or won't do in Mississippi. But when a South'n gentleman gets to deal with low-down no-account Yankee trail trash, why, ah guess rules and good manners go out the winder. Thet how it is in this forsaken north land, Daddy?'

'Why, ah do believe you might just be right, son,' mouthed Smith, his gnarled face flaring with hostility as his fingers brushed the hickory stock of his saddle rifle. 'Doubled our fee then ends up welshin' on seein' the deal through. Yessir, Yankee Doodle trickery if ever ah struck it. Well, sir, Mr high and mighty skunk-skinner, you better understand you've tried diddlin' with the wrong people. Ah consider our contract's bin violated, so kindly return my five hundred ah paid over in good faith.'

Ransom nodded. No shadow of doubt in his mind now. They'd planned this play all along; he'd just brought the hour of reckoning ahead by a day's ride was all.

He backed up slowly in the gloom until the stone outcroppings loomed on either side. This could prove advantageous. But a quick glance over the shoulder revealed there was nothing in back of him but a sharp drop into deep shadow. Maybe he'd made an error in getting off Blue, but he still wasn't too concerned. Not with his hand now wrapped round the smooth nutwood handle of his Colt .45 he wasn't.

'Close enough!' he rapped, the ring of outdoor authority in his voice. 'Don't start anything you can't finish.'

He expected them to obey. But the Smiths were expecting confrontation, were primed and ready for it. At a grunt from their father, the sons spurred their cayuses forward, plainly intent upon herding Ransom over that drop into thin air.

He was startled by the speed of the attack, but not rattled. In one blurred motion he swept Colt from leather and shot the elder brother's Cheyenne paint square between the eyes.

The sound of the gunblast seemed shockingly loud, setting up a batting of echoes that back-grounded the blurring sequence of events which followed in a rush. With the slain horse going down on its jaws with a sickening smash of bone, the rider was flung violently over its head. It was accident, not design, that saw the man bounce off unyielding stone and slam into Ransom's extended leg, jarring him off balance and inadvertently saving his brother's life.

With the second son coming at him at the run, fumbling for his gun and mouthing buck-teethed curses, Ransom was solid ready to blow the bastard out of his saddle, then finish off the other two, if that was what it took.

But his off-balance shot missed the head and the bullet ripped through the rider's shoulder causing him to corkscrew out of the saddle and nosedive to the ground, his face an awful, sudden white.

Next moment the elder brother claimed Ransom in a headlong dive and they went rolling and threshing towards the granite rim.

'Finish the varmint, boy!' Smith's frenzied shout knifed out of the deepening gloom, lancing through the wounded brother's high-pitched howls of pain that would raise the hackles of a cast-iron bear. 'Remember what the Yankees done to us at Mechanicsville. Take his giblets and guts, son, we Mechanics is right in back of you!'

Judson Smith was telling no lie. He was right in back right enough – 'way back. But there was no lack of combativeness in Ransom's husky adversary, who was swarming all over him. Much stronger than he looked, the elder brother Smith was a dirty, knee-gouging brawler who plainly knew his way round a roughhouse, and was smart enough to pin Ransom's gun arm to his side as he continued to force him backwards towards that yawning drop.

But a new element entered this fracas. Ice-cool and lethally confident before, Ransom was now quite suddenly mad clean through.

A vicious pistoning knee snapped into the Smith's breastbone, and his grip was broken. Ransom stared into the agonized, white-trash face, then crunched it viciously with a forearm jolt that sent teeth and blood spraying. Smith hit rock hard. He had no time to move before Ransom stamped on his face with his heel and twisted.

Bones snapped and the man shrieked in agony. Ransom was unrepentant.

You had to make sure they remembered the pain.

A shot flared, orange and wicked from the trail. The bullet fanned Ransom's cheek with the airwhip of its near passage, caroming off a granite pillar in back of him. He couldn't see Daddy Smith at all now, but realized that with the final fire of the set sun glowing directly in back of him, the man with the gun suddenly had him silhouetted.

He whirled and jumped, a second slug snoring harmlessly overhead as he plunged into the gloom. Bracing himself for impact, he still hit with enough force to belt every last breath from his lungs. The impact snapped his head to one side, smacking something solid. Granite solid.

Sprawled semi-conscious amongst scattered rocks and thorny brush, Ransom fought the dizziness as he squinted upwards with the heavy .45 still clutched fiercely in a skinned hand. The wind hissed and squabbled in the brush. He heard nothing for a time until he imagined he heard the sound of fading hoofbeats. A little later – whether he'd drifted off or not he had no idea – there came the distinct sound of voices drawing nearer above; nothing imagined about this.

Clutching the cocked sixgun with both hands,

he held the weapon directly above his face at arm's length, the foresight trained unwaveringly upon the barely defined rimrock twenty-five feet above. If a head showed against the early stars he would blow it off. He had no way of knowing how long it was before he heard the voices again. His eyes stretched wide in the darkness and for the first time his finger slackened off the cold metal curve of the trigger. The cautious murmur of the male voice betrayed no Mississippi twang, and the second voice was definitely female.

Ransom cursed and sleeved his forehead. He must have hit his head harder than he knew. He was hearing things. Wasn't he?

Then: 'Are you hurt?'

A young woman was leaning over the rimrock and staring down at him with moonlight in her hair. And she was beautiful.

THREE

CAGED

In the chilly still of the jailhouse morning the brutal clatter of the heavy six-inch steel key being dragged hard along the bars of Buck Conway's cell sounded as shatteringly loud as a .58 caliber Gatling Special opening up at close range.

'All right, jailbird!' bawled the ugly little turnkey, dwarfish, big-nosed and grinning in the new light of day. 'Git up, get dressed and let's git downstairs on account the marshals sure ain't waitin' all day on the likes of you!'

The half-awake prisoner exploded from his hard cell bunk, clad only in faded long johns. His eyes were wild with rage and his lean right arm shot between the bars like a striking rattler, clutching for a scrawny throat.

But the turnkey was no longer there. Having been assigned the cell-block detail at Plainsville Courthouse ever since the marshals first came to town, he knew all the tricks. He now stood taunt-ingly inches beyond the prisoner's reach, grinning like a gargoyle, delighted by the reaction to his little bit of fun.

'Tut, tut there, pretty boy,' he cackled, wagging a gnarled finger. 'Temper, temper. Better get your-self dressed and cool off afore you face Mr Needham and Mr Bourke. You show up in this mood and you're liable to get 'em sore. And that could lead to 'em decidin' to swing you right off like they done Hackett . . . fergit about a trial.'

Buck Conway dropped his arms to his sides, chest heaving, eyes still smouldering. A handsome and well-made man in his late twenties, he was recognized as Plainsville's biggest catch since the formidable team of Needham and Bourke had been assigned to the High Plains outpost a year earlier by the Territory Marshal's office.

Most of the publicity accompanying Conway's arrest stemmed from persistent rumors linking him with the notorious Mechanics outlaw band. The intriguing aspect of his case was that the two Stageville hardcases alleged to have been slain by Conway down in Harmonica had been definitely identified as Mechanics, giving rise to speculation that the shootout might have simply been a case of thieves falling out.

The marshals were determined to swing him for that double killing but the case was bogging down due to their failure to come up with evidence conclusive enough to convince a jury of his guilt.

So frustrated had the marshals become in fact

that they'd spent the past several days in Harmony, Stageville and the surrounding regions in an exhaustive search for such evidence. Now they were back and Conway was about to discover what, if anything, they'd come up with to use against him.

He quickly brought himself under control. He was convinced the turnkey hated him because he was good-looking and widely admired while the key-jangler was too flamboyantly ugly to be anything but lonesome.

'Your time's coming, Quasimodo,' he jeered, climbing into his pants. 'When I'm out of here, and it'll be soon, I'll be back to square accounts with you. I'll mash you like the dung-eating lizard you are, and—'

He broke off as the turnkey thrust a set of leg-irons between the bars and dropped them with a great clatter to the cell floor.

'Git them on, and these here manacles too, butcher boy. And save your mouth for the marshals. They love it when you mad dogs bark. It makes 'em appreciate the job they do in riddin' the ground of the shadow of the likes of you and your kind. Move, you backshootin' phony! You ain't playin' to no gallery now, flash-ass.'

Conway was quiet after that. A man shouldn't waste his energy on nobodies like the turnkey, he mused. Better to save yourself for the marshals. He might hate their lawmen guts, and would give an arm to get to dance on their graves yet he had to concede that they were at least enemies worthy of his mettle. Singly or in tandem they could scare the living shit out of even the hardiest con, if you let them.

Manacled, leg-chained and led like a dog on a leash by the jailer, Plainsville's headline prisoner quit his cell and shuffled along the spotless passageway for the stairs, passing adjoining cells where a rumdum and a stage bandit peered out at him in pensive silence.

They descended to the courtroom, a great, echoing chamber seventy feet long by forty wide and lighted by twelve outsized windows front and back with nothing but high rifle ports at either end, both to admit the light and for defensive purposes should the ungodly ever attempt to mount an attack upon the center of justice.

This had happened once, before the marshals' time. These days it seemed the gangs were so busy keeping one jump ahead of the law there was no time for organizing grandstanding assaults upon the nerve center of law and order.

Yet rumors persisted that Conway's people might try and break him out, a threat the marshals chose to dismiss. Security at the courthouse remained tight but no more so than usual. Plainsville believed the marshals might be taking the rumors of Mechanic connections with Conway too casually. Maybe they were. Nobody ever knew what was going on behind the inscrutable features of Needham and Bourke. Played their cards close to their chests, did the county's two-man team of gang-busters. If and when they apprised the public on courthouse matters it was mostly confined to their successes of which there had been plenty since they'd come to clean up the county once and for all.

A pair of trusties in the exercise yard turned to stare as Conway jingled his way into the courtroom. They traded looks and shook their heads. They thought he was a goner. Their reaction didn't even dent his assurance. He knew law almost as well as he did crime. He was full of confidence, although still bitterly regretted showing weak before these tinstar sons of bitches the morning they skywalked Hackett. Another one he owed them.

At the rear of the chamber stood the judge's bench on a low dais, the jury box on one side of this, and on the other the witness stand and a railed-off enclosure where the clerk and other court officials had their desks.

The prisoner inhaled and sneered. You could almost smell the rectitude and righteousness here. The self-satisfied, piss-and-corruption stink of the place.

They passed through by the iron door that led to the armoury, where rifles, sixshooters, shotguns and munitions of warfare were stored for emergency use when the marshals mounted posses, or should the hellions ever jump the fence.

They came outside again and across a meticulously maintained paved quadrangle in the geometrical dead center of which stood the marshals' office surrounded by immaculate petunia beds, with Old Glory flapping gently at the masthead high above a gleaming metal roof.

They were half-way across when a ragged cheer broke out. Conway jerked his head in the direction of the high grille gate and sentry boxes giving on to Front Street. He was astonished to see a small bunch of seedy-looking citizens waving and cheering. As he paused to gape, they set up a chant:

'Free Buck Conway! Free Buck Conway now!'

His chest swelled with pride. He'd always enjoyed popularity most everyplace he went, and the county seat was proving no exception. But this surely was something special. He might have shouted back had not the turnkey given a vicious jerk on his lead chain.

'Come on, no lollylaggin',' the man mouthed officiously as he hauled him up the steps. 'By glory, you'd think people had better things to do than loiter around rootin' for the likes of you. Don't they know what you done?'

'I'm an innocent man, Quasimodo. I never fired a shot that night. It was the gunman in the dark who cut those jokers down, like I told your stinking bosses.'

'And they don't believe you no more than I do.' A deputy opened the double doors to the inner sanctum and Conway was hauled roughly inside. Then: 'Here he be, your honors. Mr Buckley Conway, and iffen I might say so, the sorriest piece of Southern shit I ever did see.'

'That will be all, turnkey,' a deep voice intoned. 'Now get out and stay out until you're called for.'

The man scuttled out like a craven cur, leaving Conway standing alone on the highly polished cedar floor of a huge and light-filled cedarwood office.

Conway was impressed. Didn't show it of course. But still couldn't help it. He'd finally made it to the big time, this gleaming room assured him. Only the top hellions ever made it into this room. That was something to brag about in the future, that's if this fine pair of Federal bloodhounds didn't get to introduce him to Madame Hemp between times.

'Where is she, Conway?'

Bourke didn't look up as he spoke. He was fashioning a cigarette with strong blunt fingers.

'Who?' he replied innocently.

'Your wife,' stated Needham, a tall and lean-bodied man of fifty with the piercing eye and hooked beak of a peregrine falcon. 'Mrs Laura Kathleen Conway who was with you at your residence in Harmonica the night you murdered two men then fled from the law. We want to know what you have done with your wife, scum.'

A slow smile stole across Conway's face. So they hadn't caught her. Which virtually guaranteed Harry had carried out his instructions and spirited her away safely where the bloodhounds of the law might never sniff them out. He felt ten years younger and wanted to shout. But he didn't. Just meeting Needham's fixed stare, even Bill Hickok might well feel his gonads contract.

Both lawmen began speaking at once, accusing, cajoling, threatening and reasoning by turn.

Conway was immune. He was floating on a cloud of optimism. They had not found Laura!

The crime of which he stood accused had been committed in Harmonica where he was living with his new bride. Two hard men from Stageville came to Harmonica by night, armed and dangerous and apparently looking for Buckley Mason Conway, a local identity known to the law. In the resulting mêlée at the house the pair were gunned down from behind, their sixshooters still in their belts when the law arrived.

Although several citizens saw the strangers approach the Conway house, and could swear that Laura was with him on the balcony immediately prior to the gunplay, none had actually witnessed the shooting.

Conway insisted a third man was involved. The killer. But this statement wasn't made until a full week later. For before the authorities could arrive at the death scene, Buck and his bride fled and remained at large throughout that time despite the massive manhunt mounted to run them down. Convinced Conway was the killer of the Stageville pair, Plainsville threw all its considerable resources into the manhunt, but dashing Buck – cheered on by most of Harmonica which regarded him as nothing worse than a high-living extrovert who'd brought their town a lot of excitement – proved more difficult to find than the honest man in the Bible.

He might well have made it safely to Mexico, or even clear to South America, but for Dixibelle

McSween. Desperado and buxom blonde chanteuse had been an item on and off prior to Conway's sudden marriage, and something prompted him to visit her in the middle of a dark and stormy night illuminated only by the bright candle Dixibelle kept burning in her window for him just in case the marriage didn't work out.

In the frenzy of detective work carried out by the authorities during that previous exhausting week, Marshal Needham's lieutenants had collected everything available on their fugitive: names, connections, habits, weaknesses, strengths, everything they could get. They assembled a fat dossier, one item in which was the name, address and strange sexual proclivities of one Miss Dixibelle McSween of Cross Hollow.

Dixibelle was subsequently staked out. Conway showed. The possemen came in on him like an avalanche. The press trumpeted the capture and Bourke and Needham were photographed standing triumphantly on either side of a chained, hogtied and chastened Buck Conway on the courthouse steps at Plainsville. It was all over, the *Nebraska Times* applauded. Bar the trial, that was.

But Conway knew his law, and as a consequence proved both calm and articulate about his situation after they locked him up. Naturally he regarded his capture as a major setback, yet viewed the fact that his wife hadn't been with him at the time of his arrest, and remained at large, as a sure sign that his guardian angel was hovering over him.

Despite chains and deputies with big guns he proved able to get a message through to one Harry Duval, an associate who owed him big time. As a consequence, Laura and loyal old Harry vanished as if the earth had opened and swallowed them whole.

It was not until the manhunt for Buck Conway ended, and he was securely bottled, locked and bolted in their cells, that the marshals' legal advisors regrettably informed that, despite a wealth of circumstantial evidence against the accused, a conviction was unlikely without the vital testimony of the single eye-witness. But Mrs Conway was nowhere to be found.

Small wonder they were going so relatively easy with him today: 'Have a mug of coffee, Buck.' 'We're really your friends, Conway, don't look upon us as enemies.' And, 'Look, you know you're guilty and so do we. The jig is up for you, but you have to think of your bride. We have fifty men in the field right now searching for her, son. Who's to say what could go amiss when they catch up with her? Scared girl like that . . . weary deputies with itchy trigger fingers. We could have a tragedy on our hands, Conway. But you can prevent that just by answering a simple question. You want your bride to live, don't you, son?'

'Sure do – daddy,' he said with a grin at Needham. 'And I'd tell you if I knew, honest.'

Needham came out of his chair with snarl, and the big bony fist ornamented by two heavy silver-and-turquoise dress rings smashed into Conway's face and knocked him half-way across the office on to his back.

'You dirty, murdering piece of filth!' the lawman raged. He was going after him again until adroitly blocked off by burly Bourke.

'Easy, Needs, steady.'

'Yeah, easy, you lawdog bastard!' Conway mouthed thickly. He'd shown weakness in front of these men once, but was mad-dog fierce now as he struggled upright, spitting blood and cursing. 'You're sore because you've lost out, lawguts. You ain't got a witness and you'll never have one. You can kick the shit out of me but you can't convict me, and doesn't that gripe your everlasting soul!'

'Maybe we don't even need that witness, scum,' Needham said, back in control now. He tugged down his leathern waistcoat, towering half a head above tall Conway. 'We are closing on the Mechanics. And when we nail them, we'll have enough on you to hang you a dozen times over.'

The blood drained from Conway's face. He hadn't known they were aware of his links with the notorious Mechanics. The gang of Mississippi outlaws, who'd named themselves thus in honor of the Battle of Mechanicsville in which friends and kin were supposed to have fallen, had attracted increasing notoriety as they raided northwards through the eastern foothills of the Rockies in recent times, plundering and killing in the name of Southerners' revenge for their defeat in the War Between the States.

The Mechanics were a hate outfit, and Buck

Conway had been welcomed into it with open arms, despite his educated wealthy Georgian background which contrasted with the lowly white-trash status which characterized the majority of the marauder mob. For when it came to hate, he could hold his own with the South's best, or worst. But he was also highly ambitious, nurtured his own secret plans to make use of the wild bunch to elevate him eventually into a position of real power here in the county. There was a deal more to Buck Conway than a handsome head, a ready smile and quick gun.

'Never heard of them,' he stated, poker-faced.

'We know you're just plain scum, Buck,' Bourke said in his avuncular way, pouring the prisoner a drink in a water-glass. 'And you're South. But why would you hate the North? You didn't even fight in the war, boy.'

'Don't hate anybody, don't know any gangs,' he lied. Why should he explain anything to these bluecoat sons of bitches?

'We happen to know,' Bourke said abruptly, bushy black brows coming down to hide his eyes, 'through our intelligence arm that the men you murdered were professional killers riding with the Mechanics. We also suspect, no, we are virtually sure, that you were involved in that outfit. We're guessing they came to visit you, thieves fell out, and you murdered them.'

Conway was impressed. They were dead on target. He stifled a yawn.

'If you gents ever weary of hounding innocent

folks for a living, you could take up writing dime novels, the imagination you've got.'

'All right, you can go,' Bourke said wearily.

'Sure, we're through for now. Almost. . . .' Needham moved casually to the large colored wall-map of the region occupying one wall and continued to speak as though thinking aloud. 'Girl raised in sight of the mountains. All her life spent in view of the Rockies, in fact. Hears stories of people vanishing in the Rockies at her momma's knee. And now this young woman is running herself, I just wonder where she'd make for. . . ?'

Conway really had to struggle to preserve a poker-face now. He didn't quite manage it. They'd second-guessed him. That was how good they were. He waited tensely for what was coming next. It proved exactly as he feared.

'We've decided, in light of your continuing lack of co-operation,' Needham said with some relish, 'to recall all our search parties, resupply and rebrief them, then dispatch them to the mountains. I'll be taking personal charge of the hunt for your wife up there, you'll be excited to know, vermin. And you would probably agree that I know the mountains here better than any man living, and that my record in weeding scum like you out of there is second to none?'

'I'm hungry. You got anything here a man could eat?'

'Turnkey!' Bourke yelled. And, waiting for the man to enter, surveyed the prisoner with almost genuine disappointment. 'You're out of your class,

Conway. We'll find your wife and we'll use her testimony to secure your conviction, assure your execution.' He paused deliberately. 'But if you were to co-operate with us we might still do a deal.'

'Let's go, Quasimodo,' Conway grunted, and led the turnkey outside, where the sun was shining and a few stragglers were still visible in the distant gateway.

Again they cheered, and he raised manacled hands high. He was young and busting with life and the day was beautiful.

'Don't give up on me, folks!' he shouted. 'They'll never get to hang an innocent man!'

The turnkey swung a kick at him and voices howled their disapproval.

Standing at the doors, Bourke murmured, 'You don't suppose he's cleverer than we calculate, Needs?'

'He's a nothing.'

'They say his wife is really something though. Pure-bred quality.'

'She's a whore. Only whores cohabit with that breed.'

Marshal Bourke studied his partner quizzically. He himself hated the outlaw breed like poison. But Needham's enmity was so much stronger that hatred was not a strong enough word.

FOUR

THE SCUM ALSO RISES

The fire in the hearth crackled amiably.

'Will you please fetch me more warm water, Harry?' she said. 'I'm not hurting you too much am I, Mr . . . I mean, Jack?'

'No,' Ransom said honestly. He'd soaked up plenty punishment in that twenty-foot tumble at the rocks but nothing was broken, just a mess of cuts and bruises. And he had to admit that the dark-haired young woman, Laura, was displaying a real gentle touch as she dressed the bruising on his back, which Harry insisted was the size of his hat.

The couple hadn't furnished second names as yet. That was OK by him. He was just damn grateful they'd come along to find him even if he did suspect Harry hadn't really wanted to investigate the shooting. But his companion had insisted.

Ransom was frank about what had taken place, saw no point in being otherwise. The woman appeared to accept his story on face value but her bewhiskered companion seemed even more nervous after hearing about the Smiths than he had beforehand.

Jack scowled.

He kept thinking of the couple as 'companions'. He figured if they were husband and wife they'd have introduced themselves as such. He sniffed. He could be judgmental in certain situations. He doubted it was an attractive trait. He couldn't help that. But what was a man to think? A gray geezer who wouldn't see his forties again, and a raven-haired knockout who couldn't yet be twenty-five, sharing accommodation in a lost mountain valley miles from civilization. How many ways could you read a set-up like that?

As the warm sponge moved gently over his naked back, Ransom shook his head. He was at it again: standing in judgment. And what did that ever get a man? he asked himself severely. Lonesome, mostly. And lonesome could sometimes drive a man to taking on fool jobs he would not normally consider, simply to get away from life and people and pleasures other men found as sweet as sugar on a stick.

So he forced himself to keep on talking, informing them about the Range, his partners, the price pelts were fetching this season. He even recounted the tale of the by now legendary horse race, but made no mention of the unwelcome nickname that that victory had bestowed on him. Yet thinking on this made him wonder, considering the shootout with the Smiths, his survival, and the Good Samaritan intervention of the couple, if 'Jack the Winner' might not well be proving an appropriate tag yet again.

Laura actually laughed when he described his undignified and bruising survival journey through the brawling rapids of the upper Whitefoot in midwinter. Harry just sat staring moodily at Ransom's gunrig hanging on the doorknob of the larger bunk room.

'Relax,' Ransom felt obliged to say to the man as the young woman carefully strapped his upper chest and back. 'I really am Jack Ransom, mountain man. That's all I am. I guess that living alone up here in the wilds you'd be leery of strangers, especially someone you know has just been mixed up in a gunfight. But you've been swell to me and the least I can do back is be straight with you. So you can quit fretting, Harry.'

His reassurance appeared to take, at least for the time being. Laura put her medicine kit away and Harry brewed coffee. Ransom moved gingerly about the snug little room, flexing his upper body and trying to work the stiffness from his right leg.

'We're, ah, sorry about your horse, Ransom,' the man ventured after a silence. 'Reckon you might find it again?'

'Maybe. He's a good horse, Blue. . .' His manner was a little vague. Seated fully in the lanternlight sipping her coffee now, he realized belatedly that Laura Whoever had to be one of the finest-looking women he'd ever seen. He fought down the impulse to sniff disapprovingly again about the set-up here. Even so, he mused, you'd think a looker like that could do better for herself than wind up in a shotgun cabin half-way up the Rockies with your only neighbors bears and coons and the occasional marauding outlaw.

Which gave rise to a thought. 'These men I guided up. They were set on getting to Ghost Mountain even though I told them there's nothing up there. Any notion what attraction there might be there this time of year?'

He saw the quick glance which passed between them before Harry shook his head. Nope, no idea.

Ransom let it go, realizing that the exhaustion was catching up with him in a rush.

They insisted he stay over, and he readily accepted. He could have 'Laura's room', he was told, and she busied herself making things comfortable for him. She set out the things he might need, water, two fingers of whiskey and a painkiller should he wake up hurting.

He expected to drop off the moment he hit the pillow. It didn't happen. His window overlooked the valley to the north, and a cold white moon turned the landscape to silver under the moving skies. He saw the trees turning in a wind he knew would still be very cold up here, even in the summer season.

Vague reflections on the day's events occupied

him as he stared off beyond the black and ragged tree line to a strange needle spire of stone atop the valley wall, which Harry called Hightower.

It was characteristic that he had no regrets about the bloody incident with the Smiths. He was a man who played the game hard, had been fully aware he might trigger off some kind of showdown when he announced his decision to quit. What was surprising was the realization that he wasn't thinking about reporting the Smiths to the authorities when he returned to the Whitefoot, even though he believed in strict adherence to the letter of law. Nor was he too worried about his good horse, and whether the Southerners might have caught it and taken it. It could well be that Blue was hurt, maybe was out there right now in the cold mountain night, thinking his master dead and gone. Not caring about him.

Instead his thoughts kept returning to the woman. He could smell her scent on his pillow. He blinked at the moon and relived the touch of her fingers on his skin. Slow, even breathing filled the room and Jack Ransom slept peacefully in this deep night, in this quiet room, towards the heart of the summer. And didn't stir till morning, something unknown for this man of the mountains.

He had no notion why this should be so.

Among the trees behind the outlaw camp in the place called Glacier Canyon, the morning birds were busy where the tough new summer grasses grew strongly around and through the talus heaps.

Where the tree fringe abutted the open half of the basin, there rose a looming rampart of ironstone, atop which, 200 feet above the floor, stretched a cap of green with slender little pines and clumps of berry bushes ripening in the sun.

The brown bear moved with slow and methodical purpose across this cabin-sized patch of green, indifferent to the dizzy drop to the floor surrounding him on three sides. It paused to tear violently at the shrubs and earth, hurling the ripped turf in every direction, then dropping flat on its belly, snorting and burying its face in the soil. It was hunting ground squirrels, but didn't find any. Morosely it rose to its hind legs and stared down at the tiny moving figures by the spring, twitching tufted ears as the sound of a shot carried up to its hunting ground and beyond.

The rat-featured man sporting the crossed-swords emblem of the Confederacy on his turned-back hatbrim, lowered his smoking pistol and squinted at the squat boulder fifty yards distant. The coffee-tin still sat atop the rock, lid up, totally untouched by flying bullets.

He started in cussing his marksmanship but cut off sharp when he saw Pickett glance his way. The leader's raised eyebrows told him to cut the racket, while the hard set of his mouth added that he'd better if he knew what was good for him.

'So,' Pickett said, as the gun echoes faded, 'how are your boys this morning, anyway?'

'They'll live, I guess.' Judson Smith's expression was sour as swill. 'Stinkin' Yankee scumsucker. One boy with a busted shoulder, the other with a busted face. A man shoulda—'

'What'd you say this joker's name was?'

'Ransom. Hired him down at Tracktown. Loves hisself somethin' fierce, so he does. Hard bastard, but—'

'And good with a gun, huh?'

'What makes you think that?'

'Stands to reason. You and your boys planned all along to jump him at trail's end anyway. You were full prepared and he wasn't. Yet when you jumped him he stands you off and mauls you up pretty bad. Gotta to be good with a gun. Right?'

'The hell with that !' Smith glared around angrily. His arrival at this outlaw's Shangri La had been overshadowed by yesterday's violent clash with their Whitefoot River guide, twenty miles south-east. The awareness that he and his sons hadn't been up to the task, and that Ransom had bested them at odds of three to one against didn't cheer him any. Yet as he stared round with his pale cold eyes, he was quickly coming to realize there was definitely a bright side to this situation in which he now found himself.

The Mechanics were both a far bigger and much more dangerous-looking outfit even than he'd dared hope to find.

He estimated there were upwards of thirty to forty heavily armed men moving about sluggishly, fixing chow, cleaning their guns, attending their horses and rigs. A number were scrawny, dirty and feral-looking, but as that description fitted the

Smiths themselves to a T he found this reassuring. However the majority of the bunch were of a huskier stamp, evil-looking and hostile, sure, but that was what this mob was all about, surely.

Judson Smith harbored no illusions about his new associates. Pickett might well be notorious for his anti-North rhetoric, and the press liked to label him as a disaffected Southerner who didn't accept that the hostilities were over. But Smith had been following the Mechanics' crime spree for a time now and reckoned he understood exactly what their motivation really was. He reckoned them as nothing more than straight-out outlaws just like himself, and tabbed all Pickett's windy rhetoric about avenging the 'treachery of Appomattox' and salvaging glory for the flag as simply a recruitment gimmick to attract new members and to give the younger ones something extra to fire them up.

Deciding to link up with the outfit if possible, he'd been lucky enough to glean sufficient information on the band's movements through the owlhoot grapevine to enable him to get a fix on their hideaway here under Ghost Mountain, and subsequently make contact. So his boys were stove up and griping today. So what? Judson Smith was in robust good health and felt he'd reached some kind of desperadoes' Valhalla here amongst so many of his kind. And best of all, Pickett had personally checked out his credentials and bidden them all welcome.

Smith's mood began to improve now and he adopted a companionable tone as he turned back to his new leader. He tried an ingratiating grin which didn't sit well on his off-centered, mean-eyed cracker's mug.

'Leroy, I know you got a lot on your plate right now, but I'd sure as shootin' like to do go after thet Ransom jasper. He's stove up, and his hoss bolted on him. Mebbe you could let me have some men to—'

'What do you think this is, mister? A poorboy outfit messin' with piddlin' wrangles? This is an army, jasper. We're fightin' us a war against Reconstruction, not playin' tiggy tag. You get that? So repeat after me – what are we and what are we doin'?'

Tough Smith was shocked by the other's abrupt change of mood. But he was simply seeing the real Pickett. Certainly losers and bums and backshooting badmen were all welcome to rally to the Mechanics' tawdry colors, but they were never the head man's pals, merely minions. Pickett was an illiterate outlaw yet understood exactly how to build and maintain a fighting outlaw outfit, and you didn't get to accomplish that by permitting nobodies to suck up to you, or by granting any favors.

'Th . . . this is an army and . . . and we're fightin' a war,' Smith blurted, wounded but intimidated. 'Er, sir!'

Without acknowledgment, Leroy Pickett swung away towards a mighty slab of yellow talus nearby that formed a natural dais. But he was delayed again, this time by a husky barbarian toting a rifle taller than he was.

'Colonel, sir,' the fellow said; Pickett liked to be called this even if he'd never worn the gray. 'Can you tell me what we're doin' about Conway, sir?'

Pickett frowned as though having trouble figuring who 'Conway' might be. But he knew well enough. They all did. Like many another enterprising rogue, Buck Conway had linked up with the Mechanics as they blazed their bloody trail northwards. Eventually Pickett had entrusted this show pony with the assignment of mapping out the Plainsville armoury, a key target on the Pickett agenda. Conway fouled up the job and began talking loosely, resulting in Pickett dispatching two men to silence him. Now those men were dead, Conway was in the slammer, and his name was mud with the 'Colonel'.

'Do?' he growled. 'We're going to let them hang him, of course. What'd you expect?'

The big man, a section commander, gave a deferential bow.

'Just wondered if you reckoned to try and bust him out so's we could get the rest of what he'd know by now about the courthouse from him.'

Pickett was massaging his gaunt jaw. 'Y'know, I hadn't thought of that, boy. . . .' Then he shook his head. 'Nah, too risky. And besides, we'd only tip our hand. Anyway, we don't need any more information than we got on account we've almost doubled in size since we first made contact with that dude. We've got the manpower to smash that Plainsville crackerbox and open up the armoury right now, with more expected to join us over the next week we're here.'

'Whatever you say, Colonel. I just figgered—'

'I do the figgerin', mister.'

'Sure do, sir, sure do. Er, you gonna talk to the boys, Colonel?'

He certainly was.

Trailed by his three lieutenants, a Tennessean veteran with one arm, a former quartermaster in Robert E. Lee's own regiment, and a sharp-featured fraud who'd never seen a shot fired in anger in combat, Pickett sprang atop the rock slab and every cutthroat, gunslinger and misguided Southern patriot assembled in Glacier Canyon gathered round in eager expectant silence.

A full minute passed before Pickett began to speak. He started off quietly, talking about the South they all remembered, a South that had never existed but in myth and imagination, a land of plenty, wealth, equality and sunshine; Pickett's South was eternally sunny.

The audience soaked it up and by the time he got to reminding both old hands and newcomers of their sacred obligation to their homeland and the ways and means by which bloody vengeance might be rigorously effected, he was obliged to shout to make himself heard above the clamor of applause.

Nor would he allow them to forget Mechanicsville. Ten thousand Confederate heroes done to death at the bloodstained hands of Generals Sumner, McCall and McClelland back in June '62 along the red-flowing Chickahominy

River, this despite the legendary heroics of Jackson, Magruder and Longstreet under Lee's inspiring command.

'The glorious dead are our brothers and we'll avenge every mother's son when we descend to the High Plains and strike like the hammer of God Almighty in the name of the living South!'

With his bruised and bloody sons by his side now, Judson Smith stared wide-eyed at the surrounding sea of faces, marvelling at the emotion Pickett was generating. It was highly infectious, this spurious patriotism.

A man who'd sooner eat dirt than show sentiment in public, Daddy Smith felt a fat tear roll down his sunken cheek as half a hundred throats bawled out chorus after chorus of 'Dixie', this despite the fact that the vast majority had spent the war years looting, dodging the draft or languishing in jail for displaying cowardice in the face of the enemy.

And gazing down upon them all, newcomers and old-stagers alike, Leroy Pickett, commander in chief of the Mechanics and currently Colorado's public enemy number one, marveled at how simple and easy it had been in the end.

During a spell in prison he'd encountered a dreamy-eyed genuine patriot who could make strong men weep whenever he spoke of Holy Mother South, the 'sullied' flag and the iniquities of the oppression of the have nots dating back to the mists of antiquity.

This crackerbox oratory made Pickett weep. He

wept at the sudden, startling realization that even a poor Down South nobody – Leroy Pickett – could attract support and generate power undreamed of if he only had the brains, courage and eloquence to tap into that magical source. Patriotism.

So he'd trailed this dreamy-eyed silvertongue around the camp for weeks, studying his techniques and learning some of his diatribes off by heart. Until the Yankees dragged his shabby role model out and shot him on charges of inciting criminal unrest and exhibiting disloyalty to Washington.

No matter. He'd taught Pickett all he needed to know and from that moment on he never looked back.

The blend of bogus patriotism and all too genuine hate for the North had elevated him from just another nobody to what he was today, commander of the fastest growing gang in the West with far reaching plans even his most rabid disciples were unaware of as yet.

He waved his long arms and bellowed. 'One more verse, boys! I wish I was in Dixie, hooray, hooray. . . .'

The chorus of voices rose up the rocky escarpments and started coyotes yipping in the distance. High atop his ironstone throne, the bear sat still as death, watching.

FIVE

GRAVE FOR
THE LIVING

'What are you doing, Harry?'

Straddling the cabin's ridgepole, telescope in hand and hat thrust to the back of his head, Harry Duval started guiltily at the sound of the voice from below. His face showed a rare irritation when he saw Laura standing by the well, shading her eyes against the afternoon sun. She was mostly at prayer this time of day, which was why he'd taken the opportunity to clamber up on to the roof with his old sea captain's telescope.

'Looking for game,' he stated. 'Larder's getting low.'

She smiled. 'You know I can always tell when you're fibbing, Harry.'

'All right then, damnit! What I'm doing is keeping a sharp look-out for geezers wearing lawmen's stars coming up through the tall and uncut. So go ahead and tell me that's not something I got to do all the time. Go on.'

The girl's smooth oval face turned sober. She still did not believe him, yet could not deny that kindly, weak, loyal Harry did spend a great deal of time keeping watch for the danger they both knew could come any day and at any time.

'I appreciate your vigilance, Harry, I really do. But I know you're not looking for the marshals today either.'

'And just how do you figure that?'

'You were looking west. If the lawmen ever come here it won't be from that direction.'

'So, Miss Smarty, what am I doing then? Riddle me that.'

'Spying on Jack, of course.'

His face fell.

'OK, so what if I am? Look, Laura, just because you seem ready to bend over backwards to take this stranger on face value doesn't mean I have to do the same. He might dress mountain style but he could still be a John Law. He's big enough, mean enough and I guess looks more like a manhunter than anything else to these old eyes.'

'He hunts animals, not people.'

'What makes you so blamed sure of that?'

'I know about people.'

'Oh yeah?' Duval wasn't buying that. For Laura had married Buck Conway, who was flasher than a rat with a gold tooth and a true desperado despite a stylish veneer. He might well be growing to love

Laura like a daughter, yet wasn't about to rely too heavily upon her judgment. 'Well I know people too, and this one has got some mighty interesting qualities for a simple fur-hunter. He's too big, too, he's got tickets on himself and he hates crooks. You only had to listen to him carry on about them Southerners to know that. The lawman tag could fit a *hombre* like that neat as an old Stetson, y'know. He's sure mighty different from any trapper I ever met.'

'I'm considering inviting him to stay on.'

'What?'

'Only until he gets better.'

Duval gestured impatiently, features flushed.

'Damnit, girl, he's been out hunting with a rifle two hours. He's healthy enough to hold a bull out. And we don't need him here.'

Laura stood gazing westward for a time before responding. 'I feel we do, Harry. We're very vulnerable here, you know. Those men who tried to kill Jack, for instance. They could still be lurking about. And you're always concerned about this unusual activity here you believe is taking place right under our noses. Jack Ransom engenders confidence. I've never met anybody who did so more. I've a strong feeling we might need him. . . .'

Her voice faded as she moved off. Duval stared after her, a nerve beginning to tic in his cheek. He too found the man from Heritage Range reassuring to have about. Yet he'd encountered peace officers who manifested that same quality, men like

Plainsville's Needham and Bourke, for example. Lawmen terrified him these days both because of the danger their coming could pose for Laura as well as the threat to himself if they found out he'd been concealing a witness in a murder case.

When Laura failed to reappear he raised his telescope again and faced west. Earlier he'd picked up a distant glimpse of Ransom following the twisting course of the creek some two miles up valley. It took several minutes to locate him again. The man was now a mere speck of movement against the green, a dot of life crossing an irregular pocket in a valley dominated by a soaring immensity of stone and framed by meadow-green shading into the darker green of forest where it broke the downward slopes.

'He ain't about to find any big game down at the creek this time of day . . . which means he ain't hunting . . . so what is the big varmint doing?'

Harry Duval was right. Elk, moose and deer wouldn't venture down to drink until towards evening. But Ransom was still hunting, in a sense. He was searching for a half-Morgan half-quarter blue horse sixteen hands high with upright tufted ears.

He was limping as he picked his way across the stones studding the quick little stream, but his leg was improving fast if still a little painful. His back, where he'd landed on the granite, was one massive ache but wasn't hindering him any.

It felt fine to be out in the open, drawing good air into your lungs and working the after-effects of yesterday's violence out of the system. As well, there was plenty thinking to be done. He had to think about why he'd fobbed off Duval's offer to sell him one of their three horses in order that he might ride on, along with why he should be feeling so damn good despite all that had happened.

He halted to stand motionless upon a sandbar where the ripples surged, eddied and died in a round pool and the slanted sunlight was warm and good upon his back.

He was reflective now. Last night, Duval and the woman had shown the courage to investigate the gunplay at the granite ridge, waiting bravely until the battered Smiths finally loped off before checking out the fight zone and finding him. He owed them for sure. Yet that still did not fully explain the buoyant feeling that had dominated him throughout the day. Curious, that.

Across the mile width of valley green, beyond the wildflower-beds and the ruin of the solitary lightning-split oak, then up the emerald wall where a toe of red stone thrust out abruptly like a stubborn bottom lip, there was a flicker of movement. Moments later the blue horse appeared, limping and bedraggled, its saddle hanging beneath its belly and bloody-mouthed where the bit had broken the skin when it tried to eat.

A light breeze ruffled the knotted mane as the animal's keen farsighted eyes focused on the figure by the creek. It raised its head and whickered loud and long.

It proved some reunion. Ransom didn't care for

67

sentiment generally, yet didn't hold back when man and mount came together midway across the floor. Right along, something had told him Blue was still alive, yet even so, he'd not expected to locate the horse this soon nor find him in such relatively good condition.

He quickly unharnessed the animal and slipped its bridle before taking it back to the creek. There he watered it and sluiced it down, used ointment from his saddlebags to treat the brush cuts and sore jaws. Blue licked his face with a sandpaper tongue and the man laughed, something he rarely did.

'Come on, old-timer, let's be getting back, there's someone I'd like you to meet,' he heard himself say, then shook his head in puzzlement. Maybe that tumble in the rocks had done more damage than he knew. He didn't even sound like himself. Must be the altitude.

They headed down valley through the woods where chipmunks scuttled in the brush and a soaring eagle glided serenely a thousand feet above.

Cut off from sight of the eastern valley, they were making good time with the man striding it out in front, laden down by saddle gear, the blue horse's head at his shoulder. Both were limping slightly; two veterans returning from the wars.

The afternoon was slipping away by the time they came out of the woods and raised the cabin. Smoke wisped from the stone chimney. The horses were in the yard and the goat was visible beyond but there was no sign of the occupants.

'Oats,' Ransom promised, and the horse bobbed its head like it understood.

Still nobody about as he entered the yard with the tumbledown fence. Ransom left the horse at the water trough and strode for the barn, collecting the oat-bucket on his way. He slipped through the half-open door and froze. It was his first visit to the outbuilding. Towards the rear of the musty room in a niche between the stalls and the grain bins, a dim light showed. The woman hadn't heard him. She was lost in prayer, kneeling at a makeshift lectern upon which a Bible lay open. A figure of Jesus occupied a niche in the wall along with some saddle soap and a tin of drench.

Ransom backed out silently, feeling very much the intruder. Harry had mentioned Laura was a Quaker, and there were several religious ornaments at the cabin. He was not a praying man himself but supposed he respected others' beliefs. He wasn't sure. Had never given the topic enough thought to form a genuine opinion.

Duval was not at the cabin. Puzzled, Ransom fed the horse before going looking for the man. It didn't take long for his keen hunter's eye to pick up pigeon-toed footprints leading off towards a kind of natural grotto down by the creek. The depth of the heel-marks indicated Duval was toting something heavy.

He heard the distinct sounds of digging as he approached a natural clearing by the grotto. Muffling his footsteps, he eased forward until the sounds of labored breathing guided him to a sycamore tree, beyond which he saw Duval up to his knees in a hole some six feet long by two wide and roughly the same in depth. A large pile of dark earth rose to one side of the pit.

The man had to be digging a grave!

Duval almost fell over in shock when Ransom appeared around the sycamore.

'Damnit man,' he sputtered. 'What's the idea of sneaking up thataway?'

Ransom circled the pit, aware of his neck hair lifting as he grew more and more convinced his first guess was the right one. But if this was a grave, just whom was it meant to accommodate?

He halted, hands on hips, tall, tense and tight-lipped.

'Start talking, mister. And don't say it's not a grave because a blind man can see it is. I'm waiting.'

'It's . . . it's in case of emergency, Ransom. You know. The shooting scrape you were in, Injuns and all that about. . . .'

He broke off as Ransom reached down and grabbed him by both shoulders to heave him out of the pit on to the grass. He shook the man roughly.

'Or maybe it's intended to accommodate strangers unlucky enough to wander into the queer cozy little life you've got going here, Whiskers,' he almost snarled. 'Is that why you live this way, damn you? A woman young enough to be your daughter, and you, stuck away to hell and gone here, and jittery as hell about something, or everything. You're crooks, aren't you? You prey on passers-by then finish them off and plant them. An old badman and his whore – a pretty brace of butchers! Come on, own to it or I'll make your ass wish it had never been born.'

'For God's sake, man, you're as wrong as anybody could be. It's for what I said: in case of emergency.'

'Liar!' Ransom shoved him hard. 'Come on.'

'Where are we going?'

'Where else? Back to her to see what lie she comes up with.'

Harry protested feebly as he was propelled into the open and bundled roughly towards the cabin. Ransom was mad, yet it wasn't clear just why he was so white-hot angry. True, he sensed something odd in Eliza Valley, but it went deeper than that. Disillusionment reared its ugly head. The notion that Laura might be involved in something criminal was brutally disturbing. The woman he'd seen kneeling at prayer some kind of crook? Shocking. Yet why should you be shocked, Jack? asked the back of his mind. You mostly suspect the worst in people and are seldom disappointed. What makes Laura Nobody any different?

He found her standing in the yard as they approached the cabin. She paled upon seeing Duval being prodded ahead of Ransom like a recalcitrant steer. Ransom kept his eyes on her face as he gave the man one last shove before revealing what he'd been doing, and demanding her 'version' of what it all meant.

He was astonished by the woman's calm.

'It's all right, Harry,' she murmured, leading the shaken man to a bench to sit down. She glanced reprovingly over one shoulder at a scowling mountain man. 'There's no call for roughness, Mr Ransom. Harry was only doing what I asked of him.'

'Your idea? Who are you planning to bury out there?'

'I'd rather not say.'

'That's the girl,' Harry panted. 'It's no business of his anyway.'

Ransom stood rigid with anger and bitter disappointment as Laura remained silent. He suspected the worst. 'Women!' he heard himself mouth bitterly, and realized he was at once enraged and perversely glad. This woman, he realized, had in a breathtakingly short space of time affected him profoundly, might have even begun changing the way in which he viewed women like her, perhaps all women. And now? Well, now he felt as if he'd been saved from himself. He should be grateful, but if that was the case, as he spun on his heel and made for the cabin, it wasn't a good way to feel.

Then: 'Jack.'

He glared back, still walking. 'What?'

'All right, we'll tell you the truth. I can't have you leaving thinking poorly of us.'

'Tell someone who cares.'

'You care, Jack, that's why you're so upset. Please don't leave. Not until I've shown you something. I think you have a right to see it.'

He kept on to the cabin to gather up his harness from the porch. He was making for the horse yard but his steps were slower; he wasn't hurrying any more. Laura vanished inside and Duval watched him saddle Blue in silence. He was heaving the saddle atop the blanket when Laura reappeared, toting a framed photograph. She crossed the yard to hold out the picture wordlessly. Jaw muscles working, he glanced down at the image of a lovely dark bride and a strikingly handsome groom, both smiling happily into the lens. The woman, undeniably, was Laura.

'So?' he grunted. 'Congratulations. You've got a husband and an admirer past his prime. Lucky woman.'

'This is my husband Buck Conway who is lying in prison on the High Plains charged with two murders. The marshals are presently searching for me as the only witness. Harry is my husband's friend to whom he entrusted the job of bringing me up here so I could not be found by the law. However, I expect to be found eventually but intend to die before that happens. The grave he is digging is mine.'

Ransom was sucking breath into his mouth. His heart thudded almost painfully. My God! he thought. She sounds as if she is telling the truth. The realization stunned him. Yet his reaction seemed as extreme as his anger had been. Everything about his brief association with Mrs Laura Conway seemed somehow larger than life, inexplicable.

'Well, son,' Harry Duval sighed at his shoulder,

'are you going or staying? If I was you, I'd go. I'm not sure a high and mighty rooster like you wants to hear the truth in case you can't handle it. And I think Laura's making a big mistake telling you anyways.' His brow puckered. 'You sure you ain't law?'

Ransom didn't hear. His eyes were locked with the woman's. He'd rarely seen such pain in a human face. He forced the tension out of his upper body, nodded slightly.

'OK, I guess I would like to hear the whole story, Laura.'

She turned and led the way to the cabin.

It was a tale swiftly told. Once committed to unfolding her strange secret, Laura Conway manifested no inclination for such conversational gambits as explanations, addenda, afterthoughts or even opinions. She told it straight, for which a silent Ransom was grateful. It was a painful story, and he'd heard many. But hers touched him deeply, though he was too engrossed by the story to question why this should be so.

The courtship of the Quaker girl and the handsome Harmonica man was swift and unexpected. Buck Conway had a rakish reputation while Laura Wilson seemed destined for a life associated with prayer and good works. They married in six weeks and used Laura's dowry to set them up in a fine house in Harmonica. A short time later two outlaws came to town with the intention of murdering her husband, who slew them both.

Fearing his reputation would prejudice his chances of a fair hearing, Conway insisted they flee. He was eventually arrested but Laura escaped the law's net, into which she might have quickly tumbled all too quickly had not Conway authorized friend Harry Duval to spirit her away into the Rockies so that she could not testify against him.

Ransom filled a pipe and lit it as Duval poured him a double rum.

He believed all he'd heard. It was impossible not to.

Laura cleared her throat and continued. Their flight was successful but her husband remained in Plainsville prison under shadow of the rope, she explained. The marshals were scouring the countryside in search of her at this very moment, and she believed they would be ultimately successful, an opinion based on their high success-rate all over Wyoming Territory. If she were found and returned to Plainsville she would be obliged to stand up in court under oath and testify that her husband had cut the two men down in cold blood, testimony which would guarantee his conviction and execution.

Here she paused. Ransom proffered his glass. Laura shook her head and glanced at Harry, seated by the fire looking like a worried mountain gnome.

'I shall not testify,' she stated calmly. 'He is my husband and I won't send him to the gallows.' Her gaze met Ransom's with a frankness that chilled. 'That is why I will take my own life if and when the marshals come. Harry is helping me prepare for that eventuality, and nothing can stop me. Any questions, Jack?'

The quiet was almost eerie. Eventually Ransom lowered his chin and shook his head. No questions. He had a feeling he'd heard it all. It would take time to digest. For the present, all he did was reach down, draw his sixgun and begin checking out the loads. Laura and Duval stared at him in puzzlement as he held the weapon on his knee, angled at the floor. Even he did not understand the full significance of this involuntary action at the moment. But in time he would.

He was silently announcing his decision to stay on and stand by her. Mountain man style.

SIX

PARDNERS

The stutter of hoofbeats caused Ransom to turn in his saddle in time to glimpse one of the finest sights a man could see – a wild mustang band in full flight, streaming over the high hills like winged joy, the very essence of a freedom which for man seemed unattainable.

They were gone in an instant and he climbed back into the saddle on this, his sixth day at Eliza Valley.

How could time pass so fast? And what in the name of all that was holy was he still doing here anyway?

He half-smiled. He knew why. He was looking out for his his friend, Laura Conway. Exactly what she was to him he could not be sure. Maybe 'friend' was the closest he dared get. Nice word that. Friend. But there were better ones which as yet he dare not consider.

He found Duval at work preparing a haunch of the elk Ransom had bagged yesterday for the pot. Laura emerged from the cabin as he unsaddled Blue, and he paused to give her a long look before dumping the saddle on the top rail of the yard fence. She had a basket slung over one arm which indicated she was going after berrying. He also knew, or at least sensed, that she was waiting for him to accompany her.

As they strolled leisurely towards the stream he told her about the wild horses. She heard him through, then pointed ahead.

'Look, that clump we checked the other day is ripe now. Do you want to pick or hold the basket?'

The scene, the atmosphere, the whole summer's afternoon manifested an almost domestic ambience of which Ransom was sharply aware. He made sure they extended the berry hunt to the full, and the light was fading before they headed back.

They were remarkably easy together; she seemed completely relaxed in his company. Ransom was also relaxed yet at the same time totally alert for danger.

He realized today that he was fast approaching a major decision regarding Laura Conway, her imprisoned husband and this bizarre life she was leading under the shadow of death.

Someone had to take command before disaster overtook this woman, and who was there to fill that role but Jack Ransom?

He didn't want today to end, but this particular afternoon in early summer came apart in a rush when the the serene tranquility of Eliza Valley was rudely and crudely shattered just on sunset.

Laura and Duval were fixing supper and Ransom taking a pipe on the porch, when the riders came yelling and yipping across the south meadow. They waved their hats and raced lathered horses through the trees like a pair of scalp-hunting Cheyenne Dog Soldiers who'd just sacked the fort and drunk up the brandy supplies.

Ransom had the lights doused and his Winchester in his hands within seconds. He took cover behind the stone chimney. The moment the loco horsemen drew into range he raised the gun and dropped a shot across their bows.

'Hold up!' he roared, jacking a second shell into the chamber. 'I mean it. Another inch closer and you're meat.'

The shadowy horsemen halted sharply, their tight-reined mounts dancing nervously upon the dew-wet grass. The limber one raised himself in the stirrups and called uncertainly: 'Jack?'

Ransom swore and lowered his weapon, eyes probing the gloom.

'Link? That you?'

'Yeehahhh!' came the piercing reply, and the pair came spurring in again at full gallop. Moments later, as a wary Laura and Duval emerged from the cabin it was to see three mountain men dancing in a circle and pounding each others' backs hard enough to do real damage.

The couple didn't know it yet but they were witnessing the boisterous reunion of the three-man fur-trapping team from Heritage Range.

The fading embers of the wagon fire were still putting up a fight against the chill of the mountain air, with the smoke tatters drawing a gray canopy over the sleeping Plainsville posse, when the camp-ground quiet of Yellow Coon Creek was disturbed by a sharp sound from the direction of the trail.

The nightwatch sentry jerked his head in the direction of the noise, warily raising his Spencer carbine. Staring across blanket-shrouded shapes in the direction of the remuda and the faint trace of trail beyond, he thought he glimpsed a hint of movement but could not be certain what it was.

He stiffened as that sound came again. It was a voice. Sounded like someone singing – he was sure he picked up the word 'Alleluia!'

That was more than enough. 'Heads up!' he shouted and had the cocked the carbine to his shoulder ready to shoot when the long striding figure of a man appeared on the rim of the fire-light, swinging his arms, the striped tail of the coonskin cap bouncing almost jauntily, bulging rucksack strapped to husky shoulders.

There were eleven rifle muzzles covering Ramblin' Brother John as he came striding in to the fire, but you'd think he was being welcomed by a guard of honor, the swaggering way he saluted and bawled: 'God be with you, buckos!' in a boom-ing voice. Then he propped and started shucking his rucksack. 'Is that coffee I smell? By God and by glory I could swallow a bucket of it.'

Bewildered glances were exchanged. The Plainsville possemen engaged in the search for Laura Conway were saddle-sore, cold and exhausted up here some two thousand feet above the plains by the headwaters of the Yellow Coon tonight. And now a crazy man shows. How did a man go about getting unsworn from this outfit?

The rangy marshal in charge demanded: 'Who the tarnation are you? You could have got yourself shot! This is a posse—'

'I forgive you!' The booming voice drowned him out. The apparition whipped off its coonskin and a mane of silver hair glinted in the fireglow. 'In the name of Him who sent me I forgive every guilt-stricken servant of Satan amongst you for persecuting your fellow man in the name of that mindless monster called justice. Now where is my blasted coffee?'

To the marshal's chagrin an impressed deputy grabbed up a pannikin and filled it with lukewarm coffee from the coals.

'May the Lord Jesus Christ bestow His sweet benediction upon you and your descendants for all eternity,' responded the preacherman, and slugged his coffee down.

The possemen didn't stand a chance. There was nothing in the manual on how to deal with a situation like this. Ramblin' Brother John, as he duly introduced himself, was 'part pastor of the Great Divide and part mountain goat' who didn't permit himself such 'sinful' amenities as a horse, weapons or even food and coffee.

81

'The Lord provides for me and in return I provide Him with souls,' he proclaimed as he paced to and fro, waving his arms and occasionally thumping his chest. 'I am the fiercest enemy that sonuva Satan ever encountered on this mortal coil, and if he believes he can conceal his perfidious campaign of corruption against God's glorious humankind up here in the high country, he has another think coming. I'll walk a thousand miles to wrest one sinner free of his foul clutches, which is why there's no time for me to dally. So get down on your knees while I shrive you and I'll be on my way up to the roof of the world again, and beyond if needs be.'

He broke off, glaring around imperiously as eleven faces stared back at him dumbly.

'Well?' he shouted. 'Great thunderblasted Lord of Creation and all the ships at sea! Are you so far gone in craven lust and jelly-backed submission to the slime of original sin that you don't even recognize your Saviour's saving hand when it's proffered you? Kneel! – before the livin' Lord smites you down you sin-sodden sons of bitches – kneel!'

The marshal was caving in. He was a tough Needham-trained manhunter, but right at this moment he was just a bone-weary man who wanted only to sleep. This madman seemed genuine, so wouldn't it be simpler to take the easy way out?

'All right, men,' he sighed. 'No harm in a little praying, I suppose. . . .'

He half-expected open mutiny as he knelt upon the ground and motioned his stunned troop to follow suit. But the men were as beat and bemused as himself and it was easier to kneel than stand on tired legs in this biting cold.

'Alleluia! Here they are, Lord, and what a misbegotten lot they be. I could make better men out of a bunch of bananas – praise the Lord. But they are Your children and therefore I also love them. So by Your grace I beseech You to cleanse and forgive, shrive and strengthen every miserable one of them and redirect them to the road to Paradise. Amen. Where's my blasted rucksack?'

Suddenly he was on his way, openly scooping up a can of tinned soup as he strode by the supply wagon. Haggard eyes followed his stalwart figure. They might have warned him of the avalanches, Indians, grizzly bears and even buffalo lurking in wait for the unsuspecting traveller.

But they supposed that any man who identified himself as the pastor of the Rockies should already know all about things like that.

Within the quarter-hour all was still again at this leisurely bend of the Yellow Coon Creek. From higher up came the faint sound of a hunting owl. Then again, it could have been someone praising the Lord.

Breakfast was a hearty affair. Duval fried up haunch strips from the bighorn Ransom's rifle had brought down the same day he bagged the elk, Laura cooking hot biscuits and laughing at the new arrivals' boasting of the skills they'd displayed in tracking their partner all the way up from the Whitefoot.

'We nigh lost your sign once or twice, Jack,' attested lean-limbed Cassidy, forking meat into his jaws. 'But with me part dog-wolf and the big feller here more critter than human, we picked it up again every time.'

'Wasn't trying to lose you.' Ransom stood by the window nursing a mug of coffee. 'So, howcome you came after me anyhow? Or did they kick you out of Tracktown, maybe?'

'Like they could do that,' big Dusty Hush snorted. He paused to savage a biscuit, turning serious now. 'No sir, pard, what got us up and running was when we heard them Smiths was accused of killin' a man at Busbee, and the law posted a two hundred dollar reward on the three of them.'

'We was afeared they might jump you,' affirmed Cassidy.

'They did,' put in Harry, and proceeded to furnish details of the shootout at the granite pocket.

The partners listened owl-eyed.

'Dirty sons of b—' said Hush, then broke off in deference to Laura. But then he chuckled. 'Jumped you, huh? Bet they're sorry now.'

'You find that amusing, son?' Duval asked mildly.

'Well, jumpin' Jack's a kinda foolish thing to try, you gotta understand, partner. Ain't that so, Link?'

Cassidy nodded around a jawful.

'Plum dumb.' He winked at Laura. 'You might-n't know it, ma'am, but Jack here's about the closest thing you'd find to bullet proof and cast-iron plated. He mortal hates to lose at anythin', so mostly he doesn't. Know what they call him up on the Range. . . ?'

'What are your plans?' Ransom interrupted.

'You mean our plans, don't you?' asked Hush, leaning back and rubbing his belly. 'We're a team, Jack . . . overlookin' the fact that you quit Tracktown without even tellin' us, that is.'

'We talked her over last night,' supported Cassidy, servicing prominent teeth with a pick. 'Weren't sure then if we wanted to keep on after these crackers then. But after hearing what they tried on you, then I guess it seems a natural enough thing to do. Run 'em down, square accounts for you and pick up a bundle of cash money in return for delivering them back to Busbee.'

'Bad idea,' Duval said sharply, and the newcomers stared at him.

'Harry suspects there's some strange activity taking place over to the west of here lately,' Laura explained. 'As a matter of fact I believe you're pretty sure of it, isn't that so, Harry?'

'I've cut the sign of riders coming and going that shouldn't be around this time of year, even sighted one or two of them,' supplied a sober Duval. 'And you boys should wonder what would draw hardcases like the Smiths all the way up here this time of year? Jack, I'd stay put if I were you.'

'I'm not going after those crackers or anyone

else.' Ransom was blunt. He set his mug down and took down his hat. 'Let's get some air.'

Outside the sky was filled with light, Hightower needling a low white cloud.

Ransom fed Blue red corn nubbins from a battered tin dish and the horse nuzzled his shoulder for more. After a silence, Cassidy spoke up.

'We really want to round up them Smiths for the reward, man. But we want you along. If you want us to suck up and tell you you're the toughest in order to get you to agree, OK, you're the toughest.'

'Save your breath, pard,' growled Hush. 'That stone-jawed look of his'n says he won't do it and nothin' we say will make him. Ain't that so, Jack?'

'More or less.' Ransom felt he was letting them down. There was nothing he could do about that.

'But why?' Cassidy was persistent.

'You cain't be that dumb, pard,' said Hush.

'Meaning?' Ransom challenged.

The buckskinned hunter jerked his head in the direction of the house.

'The lady, of course. You're hooked, Jack. Knew it the moment I saw her. Never thought I'd live to see the day.'

'You are talking like a fool, mister,' Ransom said harshly. 'That's a married woman there.'

'Ain't they all?'

'Ease up, Dusty,' cautioned Cassidy, catching the glint in Ransom's eye. 'You ought to know Jack's never going to have nothing to do with no married lady.'

'Until now. . . .' Hush began, but faltered beneath Ransom's sleety stare. He turned apologetic. 'Jeez, sorry, *amigo*. I always talk too much, you know that.'

'It's all right . . . we all do things we shouldn't, Dusty,' Ransom said almost gently. And wondered just what the hell he meant by that.

Ransom said, 'Tell me about Buck Conway.'

Duval was startled. He'd emerged from the cabin to check on the horses before turning in and Ransom had appeared from nowhere, like he was waiting to jump him.

'What . . . what about him?' he said, flustered.

'Don't crap around man. Conway paid you to look out for Laura. So, that makes you his friend. Right?'

'Look, Ransom, I don't want to—'

He broke off as a powerful hand seized him by the shirtfront. Ransom's dark eyes bored. 'Is he good or bad? Killer or not? I need to know and you're going to tell me. Talk!'

Harry Duval talked. He was too tired and intimidated not to. The word-picture he painted of Laura's husband was candid, almost ugly. He didn't know if Conway had murdered two men, but did know he was a sometime crook, con man, and had almost certainly married Laura for her dowry when he was stony broke and walking.

Lightning flashed and Duval saw by its eerie blue light that Ransom appeared almost pleased by what he'd heard.

*

The storm hit around midnight as he travelled the fir slopes north of Hightower and the valley. It was one of those sneakers which built itself up to striking strength on the west side of the Great Divide and then came swooping across Glacier Canyon, Ghost Mountain and Eliza Valley to go howling and shrieking down over Skyline Plateau with such brutal swiftness that there was no chance of outrunning it.

Ransom didn't even try. He'd gone nightriding both to escape his convivial friends and to sort out his thoughts following his interrogation of Duval. Eventually he succeeded in doing this, made his decision.

'Go to the plains.'

He said it aloud to test it for integrity and horse sense. It appeared to stand up. He saw this as the only course of action for him now. They could all just sit here like scared snow hares waiting for the wolves to scent them out or the gales to blow them away, or else somebody could take action. Him. Tough enough, single minded, sometimes ruthless. Perfect qualifications for a job like the one he was mapping out for himself.

The decision once made, he confronted the big question.

Why was he doing it?

A savage gust struck them and Blue stumbled but regained balance.

The rider paid no heed as he forced himself to

come up with the answer.

He was doing it for Laura, of course. And with this admission all his feelings came flooding out, demanding to be recognized at last.

She was another man's wife and he'd fallen in love with her.

A stunning admission to make.

Shocking almost.

And yet in mere moments, in typical Ransom fashion he was accepting the unacceptable. He'd never loved before, now did so as he did everything: full-bloodedly and with an eye fixed firmly on the practicalities.

She was his responsibility now, nobody else's. And he knew in that crucial moment that he would do anything and everything necessary to extricate her from this morass into which others had placed her.

Anything and everything!

He shuddered violently as though already aware just what such an admission could entail for an all-or-nothing breed like him.

First light found both Ransom and the rain gone from Eliza Valley. But the real storm clouds were just beginning to gather for a man who'd finally found love, but in the wrong place, in his thirty-fifth year to Heaven.

SEVEN

BIG MAN FALLING

Plainsville had changed plenty in the eighteen months since Ransom had last visited. That town had comprised a courthouse, half a dozen saloons, three or four hundred citizens and the dreary look of a place going noplace in particular.

By contrast the Plainsville unfolding before his eyes was several times larger with a solid and newly prosperous look due to the telegraph, dozens of new buildings and a solid bridge across the river along with the guaranteed arrival of the railroad in the near future.

Law and order was responsible for the transformation. The extended courthouse complex and the presence of mustached marshals and lean deputies on Front Street announced this was no wild plains town any longer; the telegraph proclaimed that Plainsville was now abreast with the best.

The newcomer's interest focused on the courthouse as a weary Blue carried him slowly past. The entire complex was painted white, and the barred windows of the upstairs prison wing was visible from the street.

When he checked his horse at the Acme Livery, the man remembered him, calling him 'Mr Ransom'. He had acquaintances but no friends in the new county seat. Same as it was 'most everywhere for him.

Travelling the plankwalk for the hotel the tall figure in fringed buckskin jacket, plain flatbrim black hat and buffalo-leather boots attracted attention. Although he couldn't be mistaken for anything but a mountain man, a clean-shaven countenance combined with the intensity of his gaze and aloofness of bearing was a guarantee he was never mistaken for a good old boy or even a trapper with a fat roll on his hip ready to howl at the moon at the High Plains Saloon and Gambling Hall.

It was Saturday and Front Street was crowded with riders from the outlying outfits, ranchers and timbermen with their families, a scattering of frock-coated gamblers, painted whores and the occasional bearded, unwashed and far more 'typical' mountain man drinking up the profits of a successful season in the Rockies.

At a street junction, he glanced west between the rows of falsefronts to see the distant whitecaps seeming to float in the sky, ethereal, ephemeral-looking. But they were real enough. As she was. More real for him in truth than anything here, the planks under his boots, the stage and six wheeling by. Or even that big courthouse and jail yonder.

By the time he reached the hotel he'd collected tobacco, a newspaper and some information. Plainsville, he discovered, was still preoccupied with the killings in Harmonica, the delayed trial attracting the ongoing interest of a widely mixed aggregate of both admirers and detractors of the accused, Buck Conway.

The big-nosed clerk manning the hotel register responded readily to his seemingly casual enquiries regarding Marshals Bourke and Needham and their activities. Yes, there was a full-scale search of the mountains in progress under Marshal Needham's personal direction. Some thirty to forty men split up into smaller groups, so the fellow believed. He had obviously read the same paper Ransom had tucked beneath his arm in which it was stated quite clearly that, due to the delay in his trial, Buck Conway had become far more important than he warranted. Some factions were painting Conway as a victim of the Federal Marshals' over-rigorous campaign to clean up this county until it became the envy of all Wyoming. But both the marshals and all well-intentioned citizens, so the *Herald* proclaimed righteously, were in agreement that the accused man's wife must be found and hopefully persuaded to tell the truth about the killings in order that 'a wastrel, gunman and rogue' should receive his just deserts.

The whiskey at the Big Dipper had improved as had the furnishings and the class of the percentage girls. Ransom drank down two shots and traded small talk with barkeep and customers before making for the courthouse.

He got as far as the inner gate giving on to the compound proper, but no further. Here an officious duty deputy with an unfortunate mustache informed him brusquely that the compound was not a public facility and ordered him be about his business.

'I want to see Marshal Bourke, Deputy.' He was standing his ground. He was bigger, harder and radiated a natural authority such as this one would never be able to boast. But things have a way of evening out. The deputy was the one with a chunk of brass pinned to his shirt pocket.

'Marshal Bourke is an important man and a very busy one. What's your business with him?'

'I want his permission to visit with a prisoner.'

The deputy's eyes narrowed, the uneven mustache twitched. 'Which prisoner?'

Ransom eyeballed him defiantly. 'Conway, of course.'

'What the hell for?' the man demanded, going back a pace like Ransom had just sprouted horns. 'And just who the hell did you say you are anyway, mister? Randell, was it?'

'Ransom.' No point in lying. He was known here. 'Can I see him?'

He knew what the answer must be. The deputy was officious.

'Nobody can see that butcher. And that goes double for someone I've never seen before. Don't you know what the talk is saying these days? There's been rumors right from the outset that Conway's no-account friends might try something foolish here, like trying to bust him out. You could be one of them for all I know, jasper; I sure don't like the looks of you, let me tell you. So I recommend you hustle your ass out of here before I arrest you on suspicion. And show your long nose around here again tonight and you will be. Are you still here?'

Ransom had been told. Still he hesitated, glancing towards the barred stairway leading to the cell wing upstairs. When the deputy marshal slapped his sixgun holster for emphasis, he turned on his heel and went back out into the night.

If you couldn't skin a skunk one way you had to find another.

His initial impressions of Plainsville's mood were proving out. The town was on edge, and this tension all stemmed from Conway and the killings. Even a couple of bums, loafing by the main gate on his way out, were talking in loud voices about the prisoner as though they knew him personally. He hadn't quite decided yet if Laura's husband was either villain or hero in the eyes of the majority here, but intended finding out. Later, that was. Right now he had some weighty thinking, plus a little vital reconnoitring, to do.

He took his thoughts for a walk which led him off along Front, along the façade of the compound. The night was dark and the wind hummed in telegraph wires overhead. The telegraph had arrived at the same time as the hotshot marshals a year earlier and now spread its spidery wires wide across the plains. He wondered idly if anybody might ever be loco enough to try and sling the wire up and over the Great Divide to Idaho one day. He doubted it. But stranger things had happened. Indeed, his own presence here and the reasons behind it might fall into that so strange category. Something blocked him off from staring those reasons straight in the eye, even this late in the day. Maybe he didn't want to understand for fear he might shy and bolt in fright.

He noted everything with a huntsman's eye. The compound was well guarded but not excessively so. All that white paint and the deputies with polished badges spoke of order, assurance and discipline. Nothing hick town or vulnerable-looking about Plainsville courthouse.

A sentry smoking a cigarette stood in an alcove at the northern end of the building as the tall figure made his way down the side street. But there was no security visible as he entered the unlit street directly in back of the compound's six-feet-high rear wall.

He halted beneath an old cedar, soaked up by the night. He could see the dimly lit cell wing above the high wall from here. His mouth was dry. He was in the grip of dark emotions alien to his make-up. Having failed to gain access to Conway in order to make his own assessment of this man for whom Laura was prepared to die, he knew he had to be prepared to take any damnfool risk to do so now.

Even if it meant breaking the law.

And this was one hell of a leap for a man who'd always played the game hard yet scrupulously straight.

Then he found himself thinking out loud: 'And what if he turns out to be the shining knight Laura believes him to be, Ransom? Where will that leave you? Will that mean you'll still have to try to bust him out so he can spend the rest of his life with the woman you love?

'Of course you will, fool!' he grated out loud. And yet the words somehow sounded strained and false even to his own ear.

He shook his head and was starting off when he saw it. A disused feed barn stood facing the rear of the courthouse directly ahead. Upstairs in the hayloft he glimpsed a brief glimmer of dim light, like the glow of someone drawing on a cigarette.

His neck hair lifted. Directly above the barn's old oak beam barn hoist, where a wall plank was missing, a slender protruding object glinted metallically from the distant glow of streetlights, and he realized it was a rifle barrel.

It seemed the marshals were taking greater precautions with their prisoner than they wanted known. If that wasn't a deputy up there guarding the center of the courthouse wall in back, his guesswork wasn't worth a plugged nickel.

Ransom passed the building by without glancing upwards, shoulders hunched, weaving a little, like just another harmless drunk on the streets.

Back on Front he heard a double rye call him

loud and clear. The back street dive he finally swung into was just what he wanted; the whiskey might be rough but the liquored-up clientele proved only to ready to talk to the big stranger when they realized he was interested in Buck Conway.

Conway was a bum or Conway was a swell guy, he was told. Take your pick. The majority seemed to accept that he was a shady if engaging character who'd been heading for serious trouble most of his life. The vociferous minority painted him as just a headstrong wild boy with style to burn. It was this faction's contention that even if Conway was guilty as charged, surely he'd done the plains a favor if he'd actually blasted those two hellions who'd been subsequently proven to have had links with the Mechanics.

Leaning tall against the bar, he drank his whiskey down, inserting the odd prompt, listening, digesting, drawing conclusions. And the fact that he enjoyed it when someone vilified Conway, or hated it when he was lauded, no longer shocked or even surprised him.

He'd promised Laura he was coming to Plainsville to investigate the situation and 'see what he could do' about it. He was doing just that, but with a slant to it now, a strong bias against a man he'd never met.

Yet even with liquor and emotion working in him he was clear-headed enough to understand two things with crystal clarity.

The first was the realization that the admission

that he was desperately in love with another man's wife no longer shocked. The second was that, despite the implications of this situation, he still owed it to Conway and himself not to judge him on fallible hearsay.

He had to find out first hand just what manner of man Laura was shackled to.

It took a lot to startle the Creosote saloon. But when a deputy came in a short time later on his regular rounds, and the big mountain man from the Whitefoot hauled off and socked him square on the jaw, it succeeded in grabbing everybody's attention quick smart.

Another day in the cage nearly over. Supper burnt, and lousy canned pork, again. Nobody to talk to a man. Nothing to do but pace up and down the way he'd been doing for . . . how many stinking days was it now, anyhow? He'd lost track. No tobacco left. No visitors allowed. What were those marshal bastards trying to do to him anyway? Drive him nuts so he would crack and confess? Hell would freeze over first.

Buck Conway was at his lowest ebb since his arrest. He wanted to drag his pannikin along the bars and yell like crazy, but didn't want another licking. Then it happened. The connecting door from the annex opened and the turnkey and a flushed and flustered deputy came through with a tall and husky prisoner in a buckskin jacket between them whom they bundled, none too gently, into the cell opposite.

'You'll draw ten days' hard labor for this, Ransom,' the deputy panted, tenderly fingering a cut lip. 'Give any more trouble and you can double that, treble maybe. He's all yours, turnkey.'

'Any special instructions for this one, sir?' the turnkey called as the deputy strode out.

'Yeah. Use your own discretion.'

'I like that,' smirked the tall tough turnkey, slapping his palm with his baton. He slammed Ransom's bars viciously then headed for the annex. 'One squeak and you'll be real sorry, buckskin.'

The door clanged shut and silence fell.

Then: 'What'd you do to rile that deputy so, buddy?'

'Who the hell wants to know?' growled Ransom, sitting on his bunk with long legs stretched before him.

'You mean you don't know who I am?' Conway sounded astonished. But he wasn't fazed. Company was what he craved, unaware that it was his company Ransom wanted in turn, and had gone to extremes to get it.

'Sure . . . sure I do,' he growled. 'You've got to be the geezer who's got the whole county talking. Conway, right?'

It went smoothly from there. Conway was going loco in here, had fallen prey to doubts and bitterness recently and thus was a far cry from the swaggering man of the moment the marshals had hauled up here from Harmonica. Ransom was both a fresh ear and a news source from the

100

outside. He'd also smuggled in a flask tucked inside his boot. Conway's eyes bugged when he set the bottle in his hat and scooted it across the passageway to his door. He half-emptied it in one thirsty gulp, then hardly needed Ransom's encouragement to start in talking like a man just rescued from a desert island.

And talked and talked.

Ransom was patient initially, allowing the monologue to flow just as far and freely as the other desired. Conway was by turns boastful, remorseful, self-righteous, exuberant and bitter. Mostly he was bitter. The iron of prison had entered the man's soul. The world was his enemy and everyone had turned against him, even those who'd supported him at first now seeming either to have forgotten about him altogether or allowed the 'stinking, lousy newspapers' and 'maggot-eating lawdogs' to sway their opinions.

Have another slug, Conway. Sure, don't mind if I do, Ransom.

Subtly then, Ransom reined the man in some and encouraged him to open up on his personal life. Naturally he'd heard all about the massive search for Mrs Conway, he confessed. Was it true she had witnessed the double killings of which he now stood accused? Did Conway believe she was still alive? Could he trust her not to swear him into a noose if Needham should drag her back from the mountains?

Conway was sweating as he paced to and fro. His style had badly eroded behind bars. He looked lean, mean and desperate as he snapped off his answers to the questions Ransom posed, not revealing a great deal until that last query about whether he trusted his wife now.

'She'll never spill her guts, at least I've got that on my side,' he almost slurred. Too much liquor drunk too fast was having the predictable effect.

Ransom was disappointed. 'You trust her that much?'

'Nothing to do with trust, boy, everything to do with religion.'

'Religion? How so?'

'Everything's to do with religion with my dumb wife!' This didn't sound like any kind of compliment. Conway made a sideways chopping motion. 'I was living with two people in Harmonica, my wife and God. She knows the name of every sin there is and never commits any of them. The very worst sin to Laura and all them fool Quaker-Christians . . . whatever, is thou shalt not kill. She told me when we were on the run that if they caught her she'd have to tell the truth even if it got me hanged. Would you believe she said she would sooner die than have that on her soul?'

'Sounds like a woman in a million.'

'A fool in a million, more like.'

'How do you figure?'

'She's a nut, like all those holy rollers. But I knew she was loco-holy before I married her, so I can't gripe about that.'

Ransom was staring through the bars fixedly. 'You married a crazy woman?'

'A crazy rich woman, Ransom. Her last living kin, some old-time uncle fart, he guaranteed her this fat dowry if and when she married. A big house! I've been living in high hopes and dosshouses all my natural. Couldn't get her to the altar quick enough, I couldn't. Say . . . this goddamn bottle's near empty.' Conway blinked. 'And what are you staring like that for, anyway.'

Ransom indeed was staring. He'd never known a dead man to walk and talk before. This man, this scum couldn't be let live to threaten Laura's life, an inner voice he hardly recognized was saying. That was the immutable fact that overrode everything else. At last he knew what he must do, was easy with it now. There was no other course.

It was just like planning and executing the hunt for a dangerous animal up on the range, such as moose, wolf or grizzly. You did all the hard work first up, sitting in camp with a mug of joe in your hands and figuring exactly how to go about it. Exactly. Then, if the planning was right, you went ahead and ended up with a pelt that could buy you a month at Madam Dixibelle's in Tracktown if that was your fancy.

Now he was ready.

He didn't apprise Conway of his plans yet, didn't trust him not to foul them up. His fellow prisoner was as surprised as the relief turnkey when Ransom suddenly crashed to the floor, coughing and groaning. 'Get me a bucket, I'm going to puke!' he hollered. 'Quick, it's coming up!'

It was the gargoyle dwarf who appeared at his cell door, knuckling sleep from his eyes, half-awake.

'Judas, I'm not cleanin' up after the likes of you,' he barked, snatching up his key-ring. 'Out here, in the trough, damnit!'

Ransom's fist hit the man's jaw with a sound like an axe splitting wood. He grabbed for the gun, then the keys. Conway's eyes were enormous as his door swung open. Ransom silenced him with a gesture and led the way swiftly through the sturdy annex door the hurrying turnkey had left open, darted to the top of the stairs. Below them, a deputy stood squinting upwards.

'What's going on up there, turnkey?'

With all his strength, Ransom hurled the heavy key-ring. The man ducked but it caught the side of his head. As he stumbled, Ransom was down the iron steps like a catamount after a kid. One savage blow slammed the dazed man back into the wall, the second chopped him to the floor.

'Judas Priest!' Conway gasped. 'You're a one-man demolition squad, Ransom.'

'Shut up and follow me,' Ransom panted, plucking the deputy's key-ring free. He'd made mental notes of the cell block layout on his way in, just in case. He led the way to a sturdy rear door giving on to the shadowy courtyard in back of the courthouse. 'Back wall's unguarded,' he stated crisply. 'The street's darkest where you can see the loft of that old barn. That's the point to go over. Well, what are you waiting for?'

A disbelieving Conway tried to pump his hand. Ransom brushed it aside and bundled him out into the yard.

'I'll cover you from here then come after you when you've made it over. Go!'

Conway sped away. Staring after the receding figure, Ransom slowly raised the .45. The running man was half-way across the open ground, two-thirds.

A suppressed groan escaped Ransom's lips.

He was doing something such as he had never done before, was at war within himself and knew that Jack Ransom must be the ultimate loser.

Deliberately, he slammed the pistol butt into the hard timber of the doorframe, the sound carrying across the courtyard like a gunshot.

In the half-light he saw the running man shoot a startled white glance over his shoulder. Conway stumbled and almost lost his footing but lunged on, arms reaching for the wall. But there was movement in the shadowy hayloft of the old barn beyond, and as Conway hit the wall and sprang upwards, seeking purchase, the voice rang out.

'Halt, or I fire!'

Ransom didn't seem to breathe as he watched the desperate man claw his way atop the wall. The crash of the rifle and the hot yellow flare illuminating the hayloft caused Conway's body to twitch, like a horse raked with spur. Desperately he fought to hang on. 'R-Ransom, you double-crossing bastard. . . .' His words were swallowed by the roar of the second shot and he fell back into the yard and didn't move.

Ransom was running, hugging the courthouse's rear wall beneath the overhanging balcony until he lunged around a corner to confront a man running towards him. Ransom touched off two diverting shots that caused the deputy to falter and bar his eyes against the sixgun's flare with his pistol arm.

Coming on like an express, Ransom charged the man down, leapt his rolling body, and the gate was ahead of him.

Pinning his ears back, he took off for Front like a stag pursued by a relay of hounds. Rifles stormed and ricochets sang off stone and timber in a mad cacophony of sound behind, which bothered Ransom not at all. For the shooters were only half-awake, and he was already gone, hurtling across Front, down Willigan's Lane, then pounding round the first corner with the Acme Livery lying dead ahead. They wouldn't catch him astride Blue in the first mile nor the next fifty.

EIGHT

FIELD OF FIRE

'Dusty!'

'What?'

'I don't like this . . . it don't feel right.'

'Tell it to your girlfriend. Now hush up and stick close. We're takin' a closer look at this camp-fire and that's it. Savvy?'

There were no close trees here in the gloom beneath a darkened sky. The bare hillside the partners were bellying across was in fact a talus slope consisting of ice-chipped rock fragments, the result of endless erosion caused by frost action. Constantly sliding in a slow movement called talus creep, which only geologists could measure, the slope and its shadowy surrounds seemed safe enough to the two hard-breathing mountain men. Geologically safe, that was. Lanky Link Cassidy had serious doubts about the safety factor in human terms.

It had taken time, effort and a deal of skill to follow the trail of the Smiths from Eliza Valley here to Glacier Canyon. Arriving before moonrise they'd spotted a distant camp-fire below by the shores of a paternoster lake where a forest of brooding Engelmanns stood watch – over what they didn't yet know. It was too dark to see much of anything, which made the situation risky. Yet big Dusty Hush was as determined to make the last mile of this manhunt as his partner had been to tackle the lighthearted first.

They'd hunted wanted men successfully before in the summers when funds were running low. Cassidy kept reminding they'd never gone after hardcases as dangerous as the Smith clan before. Hush countered with the harsh logic that they were stony broke and had no choice.

Cassidy and Hush had no way of knowing just how far out of their depth they were. Three feral crackers in poor condition were nothing compared to just who and what were bedded down here in Glacier Canyon with the Smiths tonight.

'Who's thar?'

The sudden challenge, seeming to come from mere yards away, saw the crawling trappers freeze solid and hug mother earth. The challenge was quickly followed by a second voice coming from a different direction.

'Give the bitchin' password! Fast!'

'Jesus!' Link Cassidy gasped.

That wasn't it. 'Intruders! Let 'em have it!' the first voice barked, and in an instant the canyon jarred alive to the bellow of close-range rifles that blossomed like flowers of death in the murky gloom.

'Leg it, for God's sake!' roared big Dusty Hush, and was up and running with the agility of a man half his bulk. He covered less than ten yards before being smashed to the ground. Sprawling half-dazed, at first he thought he'd been shot. He then realized Cassidy had crashed into him, was lying across his body. He made to push the weight off him, then gaped in horror when he saw what had happened. A high-powered bullet had caught Link Cassidy above the right temple and blown away the back of his skull.

Sobbing with emotion, big tough Hush rolled violently away from the horror to come up on one knee with a roaring Colt in either hand. Gunflame lanced back at him from a score of points beyond the talus slope, the trapper's Colts beating heavy thunder, the angry concussions of the enemy fire coming back at him like the voices of savage hounds.

He could make out the dim shapes of running men against the glow of the camp-fire coming from far below. Holding the point of his fire low, he unleashed a final deadly volley at a trio of rising silhouettes close by, drawing gurgling howls of pain and terror as his lead bit deep.

His jaws locked with grim satisfaction. That was for Cassidy. Now it was all for himself as he threw himself recklessly off the talus slope to go plunging up the uneven bed of the arroyo where the horses were tethered. The moon looked down indifferently as he stormed away with tears blurring his vision. Whether down on the plains or here in the high country, this was proving the darkest of all nights for the partners from Heritage Range.

Five deputies were assembled beneath the blazing lamps of the communications room as the bloody-faced turnkey gasped out his report.

'It was that big bastard, Ransom. Said he was gonna puke, and I didn't wanna clean up no mess that time of night. He stunned me, but I was comin' to as they went peltin' for the stairs. Then they jumped the ground-floor deputy, and I saw . . . I mean I heard Ransom shovin' Conway out the door, tellin' him to run for it. . . .'

'You saw, but you were too gutless to do anything, you mean,' accused a deputy with a black eye and broken nose. 'All right, then what?'

'Dangest thing. Conway runs, and this Ransom bangs agin' the door, alertin' Sharkey here over in the barn. Well, old Sharkey got him good, and Conway died cussin' Ransom, like I guess he had cause—'

'Ransom's a mountain man,' the senior deputy cut in sharply, scanning the charge sheet. 'So he'll be running for the mountains like they all do.' He swung to the wall map. 'Who do we have out there?'

'Please, sir,' said a fresh-faced clerk at the telegraph desk, 'Marshal Bourke is overnighting up at Mammouth with two junior deputies.'

The senior man's face flooded with relief as he stabbed a finger at the map. 'That's the first break we've had. OK, closest access to the high country for Ransom is here, Turlock's Pass. He's making for there, you can bet your boots—'

'And Marshal Bourke's less than ten miles from the pass,' the clerk finished excitedly.

'Ten miles for Bourke, forty for Ransom,' the deputy said with grim satisfaction. 'Joe, get that key of yours working fast, and get me Mammouth, pronto.'

Dawn found Harry Duval astride the roof with his telescope, a mug of cold coffee in his fist and the worries of the world on his sloped shoulders as he stared into the slowly lightening west.

Directly below in the kitchen Laura Conway was encouraging a haggard Dusty Hush to take a little nourishment washed down with a slug of rye.

Hush looked like hell. Yet the woman found it curious that he seemed more concerned about Jack Ransom's possible reaction to Cassidy's loss than to the man's death itself now.

'You don't understand, ma'am,' he explained. 'Jack's always riding herd on us and tryin' to keep us out of trouble. He'll say this was my fault, and he'd be right.'

'You think very highly of Jack, don't you?'

'Sure. Don't you too? I mean, him going down there to Plainsville to look out for your husband and all . . . that's the kinda thing only Jack would or could do. Say, what's that?'

The noise they heard was Duval raising the alarm from the rooftop. They rushed outside apprehensively, for Hush had made it back overnight sure in the belief that the sizable bunch of badmen he'd seen camped out in Glacier Canyon below Ghost Mountain would come hunting him today.

They were relieved to see no sign of riders, just one man striding across the damp grass between the heavy oaks, swinging his arms vigorously, chin up and shoulders pulled well back. He wore a coonskin cap, carried no weapon they could see, and he was singing, his booming voice reaching them clearly on the morning air:

> For the Lord knows the way of the righteous
> But the wicked shall fall by the way
> Arise O Lord, confront them
> Deliver me with Thy great sword!

It was due entirely to Laura Conway's generous nature that Ramblin' Brother John found himself seated comfortably at the kitchen table gulping black coffee a short while later. Duval would have seen him off with his shotgun, while Dusty Hush still feared that this odd stranger might prove to be an outlaw spy from the canyon.

With a twenty-mile hike over the Great Divide's very spine behind him as he boomed out his hymns and alleluias to the icy peaks and startling feral predators, the preacherman was ravenous. He swallowed boiling coffee like it was milk tea

and was benign in the face of suspicion and hostility.

Brother John knew from wide experience that
mostly all he ever had to do in his selfless mission
to the ungodly was to get a toe in any given door
after which he would be just fine. From that point
on his silver tongue, overbearing manner and the
sheer unexpectedness of his unique blend of
charisma, excitement, fresh news and a powerful
dollop lick of down-home Christianity which he
could breathe into a place invariably proved
impossible for isolated and often lonesome people
to resist.

And he was being proven right here. Yet again.

Within an hour of his arrival he had them all
eating out of the palm of his hand. No, he had no
news of a Mr Ransom on the Plains. But he did
know Marshals Needham and Bourke had search
parties crawling all over the foothills and lower
mountains in search of Buck Conway's wife, 'In
order that they might secure a conviction against
that rascal and rope-dance him high, wide and
handsome,' as he put it.

'With apologies for my choice of words – Mrs
Conway,' he said, seeing the color drain from her
face. He hooked his eyebrows high. 'Stands to
reason if I can find you folks then those possemen
can do the same, little lady.'

So he knew already, they realized. He'd
connected one Conway name with the other and
drawn a conclusion that happened to be right on
the money.

There seemed no point in Laura trying to deny she was Buck Conway's wife. They'd not met Brother John before but his fame travelled wide, as far as Heritage Range and beyond. Their attitude seemed to be: if you couldn't trust 'The soul saver of the Great Divide', whom could you trust?

'Have you heard any fresh news on my husband?' Laura enquired, confirming the man's assumption. She added, 'Or of Mr Jack Ransom, perhaps?' Compassionately, Brother John shook his head. No. He'd been out of touch over the past twenty-four hours, was unaware of momentous events at Plainsville.

Another round of coffee and the three were ready to confide in their visitor about the night's alarming events. The preacherman turned grave as Hush informed of his partner's death and what he'd seen at the canyon.

'That would have to be the Mechanics you stumbled upon, if I'm any guess,' he proclaimed authoritatively. 'I've heard nothing but whispers and rumors concerning those vermin for weeks and I've had a suspicion they might well be high up, where it's safest. But those ungodly ones are not our main concern today.'

'They ain't?' Hush said. 'What is it, then?'

'You need to ask?' Brother John bawled, springing to his feet with both arms reaching high. 'It's praying time, sweet God Almighty. The Lord Jesus had seen you here in your misery and fear and so He sent me along to hand you a dose of His sweet love and reassurance. Sweet love and what?'

They were supposed to chorus 'Reassurance!' but were a little slow on the uptake.

'Merciful heavens!' he shouted, striding up and down. 'I can see I got here just in time on these holy soles of mine. You poor sin-begotten creatures have been locked away up here grappling with your misfortunes and vicissitudes for too long, doing what little poor weak and misguided mortal creatures that you are can to stave off the Doom and the Darkness – when what your mottled souls are craving is a dose of knee-snappin', liver-bustin' and Satan-rippin' salvation. What do you crave?'

'Salvation?' Hush was hesitant. He'd never been penned up in the same room with one of these before.

But Duval was resistant. 'Look, we don't need any prayer meeting, damnit—' he began to protest, but got no further.

'Profanity in church, brother?' The preacher-man's rugged face turned mottled. 'You dare curse in God's holy church?'

'I don't see any church.'

'Why, you poor misbegotten fool! Wherever I am is church. Holy ground. And you're here to pray for your own sorry souls. You have to shuck your sins afore the Almighty can help you. Believe me I know. I've been fighting sin all my days. I've been down in the valleys wrassling with it. High on the peaks. Up to my hip pockets in mortal sin. I've been blistered head to toe from the heat of it. But hot, freezing or tepid sin, I prevail against it and so shall you. On – your – knees!'

There was an air of unreality in the scene. These were serious, troubled people with burdened minds and genuine fears for what might lie round the corner, while this man was surely just a non-involved outsider, albeit a forceful one. They resisted, yet at the same time found themselves feeling they wanted to give in. For whatever he might be, God's messenger or perambulating fake, Ramblin' Brother John had a way about him that made you want to go along with him, if not to find salvation then at least to get to feel just a little better, to take hold of something, anything, that promised to take you out of yourself and focus someplace else other than on your burdensome troubles, if only for a while.

Laura knelt first, over by the sofa. Dusty Hush was certain he would not have buckled under that commanding stare had he not lost his best pard overnight; praying suddenly didn't seem such a bad notion at this moment, come to think on it. And after he got down, why, Harry Duval was just too weary, isolated and plain disgusted not to follow suit.

Brother John's beatific smile embraced them all. The barbarians of doubt, pain, loss and misery might be at the gates – or even real barbarians with Southern accents – but he knew what he could do for good people and straightaway set about doing it, as only he could.

'So, give me elbow room here, Lord,' he trembled, eyes on the rafters. 'We're going to sing, dance, praise Thy name and cook clam chowder

116

on stage today or I ain't the Rambler and your redeemer of lost souls. Amen!'

Marshal Bourke sprawled full length behind the blue boulder, cut himself a generous plug of tobacco and thrust it into his left cheek. Munching slowly, he moved his heavy body into a more comfortable position and lifted the heavy Sharps rifle into position.

Following the hectic ride from Mammouth to the pass in response to the urgent wire from headquarters, he was now almost relaxed, a craftsman preparing for the work he did best. He'd brought but one deputy with him, leaving the other at Mammouth to handle communications. He glanced southwards where his man was invisible in the heavy brush which crowded the mouth on that side. The deputy had strict instructions not to take part unless called upon to do so.

The man was young and untried while Bourke, at forty-six, was old in the ways of his profession.

The lawman had killed often in the line of duty and was ready to do so again if this Ransom fellow resisted arrest.

Ransom was coming in. The marshal had picked him up with his field glasses just a short time earlier. Tall and husky and riding a Morgan-quarter, was Plainsville's description of the wanted fugitive. Head office had also estimated the man's time of arrival at Turlock's Pass, and that fitted as neatly as the description.

Last night Bourke had gone to bed exhausted

from the manhunt for Laura Conway, had been due to link up with Marshal Needham higher up today. Instead he found himself here at the pass, fresh and eager for action in his understudied way. Buck Conway had died attempting to escape from the courthouse and this Jack Ransom was responsible. The eyes of the county were upon Marshal Bourke and he would not let them down.

A faint frown creased the man's brow as he stared down upon the brushy overhang concealing the trail beneath which behind the rider on the blue horse had disappeared a minute earlier as he approached the mouth proper. He'd expected him to reappear by this, by which time he would be comfortably within range of the Sharps should he be obliged to use it.

He still couldn't see the horseman but the horseman could see him.

Ransom eased his position in the saddle as sweat trickled down his spine. Through a hand-kerchief-sized gap in the vines he could see the dark blob above the rockline which was the crown of the waiting rifleman's black, chimney-stalled Stetson hat. His fingers stroked the horse's sweated neck, tracing the knotted veins there. They'd run hard and would still be running – headlong into trouble – had not Blue's mountain-trained instincts caused the animal to slow, which was sufficient warning to prompt Ransom to draw rein upon gaining the cover beneath these twin-ing overhead vines.

The horse had scented the danger and now the

man was looking straight at it and deciding what to do about it.

He could wheel about and run. Sure. But into what? He was a wanted man, and the plains would be crawling with law. So it figured, if he couldn't go back he must go forward.

He knew what this implied but flatly refused to balk at the possible implications. Just get up to Eliza Valley. That was all that signified. A man who'd always lived by the rule had discovered that in breaking the law once it seemed far easier to do it again. Laura and his pards needed him, and he needed them. End of story.

Smoothly he swung down, tapped the horse's nose to fix it in place, moved off with rifle in hand and shell belt catching the light.

There were fissures and folds in the tumbled land mass to the left of the pass which offered all the cover a hunter could ask for.

He climbed swiftly without a whisper of sound, a model of lethal intensity and concentration as he bellied round brush, snaked between rocks, at all times moving higher until he was high enough.

The man with the chimney-stalled Stetson, marshal's badge and Sharps rifle was now partially visible amongst a scatter of heavy blue boulders upon a sloping ridge directly above the pass. A bare hundred yards of slabstone, briars and scattered clumps of thornbrush separated the ridge from Ransom's position behind a lone cottonwood which puffed like a grounded green cloud atop a swaleback hill.

He squinted down the barrel of the Winchester. Sunlight danced off steel and blurred his vision. He shut one eye and took aim with the other, man and gun moulded into a single fused entity, his once strident conscience packed away and left far behind upon the streets of Plainsville.

Or so he hoped.

'Shuck that rifle, lawman!'

Bourke leapt and whirled, firing before he had a target.

The big voice of the Sharps engulfed the flatter spang of the Winchester. With gunsmoke billowing sluggishly in the still air and the echoes beating their way wall to wall up along the pass, the lawman buckled in pain before throwing his bulky body back behind an ancient stone.

Ransom levered a fresh shell into the chamber and waited.

A shot cracked sharp somewhere behind him.

He spun, astonished. The blue-shirted deputy was well away to the south on the slopes, barely within rifle range, a crouched figure behind a smoking weapon.

'You young fool!' roared Bourke.

'That he is,' Ransom affirmed, swiftly taking stock of the situation. The marshal was the dangerous one, and he was hit. If the deputy couldn't nail him at this range when he'd had a sitting shot, he calculated, it stood to reason he wouldn't get him moving. And Ransom had to move. Now. No telling how many he might be up against here.

He was up.

The deputy triggered again, but Ransom already had the fat cottonwood behind him now, protecting him from that angle. The slug smacked stone well to one side, the ricochet shrieking like a wounded bobcat.

He covered fifteen paces in a weaving panther rush through the thornbrush. Thirty, and still no sign of the marshal.

Ransom scanned the frowning caprock above, fearing what he might see. Nothing. Just stone etched sharply against powder-blue sky.

He swerved behind one boulder then sidestepped to another, sliding to a sudden halt.

Still nothing.

Could his man be dead? Another shot coughed from the south slopes behind. He ignored it. Then the deputy was shouting:

'Marshal, he's closin' in on you!'

As the reverberations of the shout faded, Ransom clearly heard a rifle lever being worked close by.

'Throw it out and we'll call it even, Marshal,' he warned. 'I don't want to kill you but I will if you make me!'

Could this be honorable, law-abiding Jack Ransom delivering a deadly ultimatum to a federal lawman? It would seem crazy if it wasn't so real.

'You are under arrest, Ransom. We know what happened in Plainsville. Surrender or I'll gun you down.'

Ransom could outwait anything on two legs or four. It was his profession. But there could be no waiting here, no delay. The game was afoot. This was a man he didn't want to fight, yet to fail here would see himself either killed or dragged back to prison. He'd come too far for this to happen now. Further than he might ever have dreamed in his worst nightmare.

He dumped the rifle and hauled his Colt. A zigzagging run carried him towards the boulders. The deputy screamed a warning. Instantly the big-bodied marshal rolled into sight with his Peacemaker clutched in both hands, firing furiously. Hurling himself to one side, Ransom fanned hammer and kept triggering even as he crashed heavily to earth on one shoulder.

Every bullet missed but one – as he intended.

With one dead man on his conscience, Ransom had discovered in those final split seconds that he couldn't do it again. It mightn't be much but it was something.

His expression was blank as he watched Bourke roll in agony, clutching a bullet-smashed thigh bone. There was no way a man in that shape could make it to the high country – and he'd have to be satisfied with that.

Ransom would not remember sliding his way down over loose rocks and rubble to reach the floor of the pass. High above, a solitary eagle glided on the thermals, flicking its pinion feathers each time the deputy's rifle barked impotently from the slopes.

Blue whickered excitedly as he approached but Ransom did not respond.

He might not have killed, yet he felt like a stranger to himself as he swung up and allowed Turlock's Pass to swallow him.

NINE

CYCLONE ALLEY

The fire was burning low. The marshal had set it
carefully in a nest of rocks where it couldn't send
up any tell-tale wisp of woodsmoke to go feathering across the moonwashed mountain night.

This was high up, much higher indeed than the
posse had intended to be by this time. Grizzly
country, Indian country, outlaw country, and no
prudent lawman or posse could afford to be
anything but cautious here in the region known as
Cyclone Alley. Men died frequently or disappeared
mysteriously in the Rockies from time to time. The
marshal liked to think that many more would have
done so but for his presence in recent times.

Tall, blanket-shrouded and militarily upright,
Needham was the last man standing at the camp.
He had five men off scouting and another three
standing watch while the rest of the posse slept.
And how they slept. Well fed if simply so on broiled

saltpork, mashed beans and a generous ration of saleratus biscuit all washed down by lashings of coal-black coffee, the dozen motionless figures muffled up in their sleeping-bags now snored on with their feet to the toasting coals.

Beyond the reach of the firelight but dimly outlined by the wash of the moon, crouched a lone cedar which had somehow survived the cyclone which had ripped across this lofty shoulder of mountainscape the year before the marshals hung out their shingles at Plainsville Courthouse.

Needham tugged his blanket closer about his shoulders, cold but not sleepy.

Bourke was overdue.

He'd arranged to meet his partner at this rendezvous after his roving scouts reported increasing sign of suspicious activity in the Ghost Mountain region, hence his forced march to the Alley. He was concerned about his partner yet not overly so. Bourke wasn't simply a good lawman, but right up there with the best.

A scout forked his bronc over the western swales to report in, weary, unshaven and stiff with the cold. The man arrived with the conviction that something big was surely brewing higher up. Nothing concrete but more than sufficient to maintain Needham's optimism. He was scenting Mechanics everyplace he travelled, and the higher he got the stronger the stink.

It was an hour later when a sentry alerted them to a horseman approaching from the south. As the man rode into the firelight, Needham realized it was Bourke's second deputy from Mammouth.

The exhausted deputy slid to ground to announce that Bourke had been badly wounded in a gun battle at Turlock's Pass by a mountain man named Ransom, who'd earlier played a major role in the attempted escape and subsequent death of prisoner Buck Conway.

Needham took the news in grim silence. He and Bourke were like brothers. Indeed the marshal seemed almost dazed by the news as he moved slowly in and out amongst the sleeping possemen, until his Shoshone tracker arrived on a lathered paint pony to report the positive sighting of a large group of men massed up at Glacier Canyon. The man also suspected the Mechanics might be aware of the posse's presence, and had appeared to be preparing for action when he quit the canyon.

This snapped the marshal out of it and set him to studying the maps with his scouts, two of whom were Shoshones who knew this entire region down to the last toadstool and bird's nest.

Needham was a study in concentration as they worked by the light of a bullseye lantern. Ever since the Mechanics had made their presence felt down in Colorado, he'd sensed they would prove to be far more than just another wild bunch. This suspicion had been confirmed by their subsequent raids, their elusiveness and their spurious claims to Southern nationalism which had attracted disaffected Confederates in numbers.

The outfit's holing up here had puzzled at first, until Needham heard of the strident declarations

Pickett was making of 'battling Reconstruction'. Pickett was scum, but no fool. The marshal took the threats seriously and the moment he did so, the significance of the Mechanics coming had grown clear.

If Pickett was envisioning a serious uprising, then he must obtain arms and ammunition. The largest source of such was to be found in the armoury at Plainsville courthouse.

Ever since this suspicion hit, Plainsville law had been committed to finding and dealing with the Mechanics before they could make their strike.

It took an hour of meticulous assessment of terrain, travelling times, conditions and incidentals before the marshal and his men came up with a name. Creation Basin. Located a mile or two below Eliza Valley and Squaw Trail, this was a highly unlikely place to mount an ambush – unless of course one knew of the scores of concealed body-holes pocking the featureless valley floor which had been dug years ago by the Indian warriors during the blood feuds between the tribes.

The Shoshone scouts predicted the Mechanics would have to travel via the basin, insisted that ambush was not only possible but success guaranteed providing he heeded their advice.

And hard-to-convince Needham totally agreed.

Iron-jawed and resolute once again, he drew his pistol and fired three shots into the air to jolt awake every deputy, critter and hootowl in the Alley.

Within the hour the column had put the Alley

behind them and were entering the pine woods beyond.

'Are you sure?' Pickett growled thickly, eyes still heavy with sleep. He blinked at his travel-grimed night scout, a gaunt and rangy figure in Confederate cavalry boots and sorry hat. 'You say you seen a lawman scout?'

The man's head bobbed. 'I was spellin' down by Falcon Spur at the creek and the bastard nigh rode over me. Forkin' an unshod pony, is why. But I hid and got a look at him good, Gen'l. It was a Shoshone sportin' Plainsville patches on his old coat. He was ridin' fast, and I tracked him back to within a couple of miles of the canyon.' He paused before adding proudly. 'By moonlight.'

Pickett was fully awake now.

'They wouldn't have scouts out 'less they was close,' he mused. 'Headin' where, you say, boy?'

'East by south, boss. Squaw Trail, Skyline Plateau, Cyclone Alley way.'

'They're a-comin' lookin' for us,' Pickett said slowly as huddled figures gathered round. 'Well, guess we knew all along we'd have to bust through all what them marshals could throw up to git to the courthouse and that ammunition dump they got there, what we need real bad. I figured to fight 'em down there, but if they've wandered up here, why that gives us the kinda edge you only dream about.' He clapped his hands. 'We'll ride at first light. And we'll wear our fightin' hats, by God and by Jesus!'

Excitement buzzed, but a Mississippi twang cut through it.

'What about Eliza Valley and that bastard Ransom there what done me and my boys, Mr Pickett sir?'

'And the geezer that killed my buddies here the other night, Leroy,' put in a long-haired desperado with a face to scare a snake. 'The scouts reckon they likewise come from the valley. So I guess we'll be detourin' there offen the Squaw on our way to Skyline tomorrow, huh?'

Pickett scowled. He had no interest in detours, delays or reprisals now that he sensed his major enemy might be close by. Not with the prospect of springing a surprise attack upon the posse in the wind, he didn't. But nobody said no to Monk, not even Leroy Pickett. Pickett prided himself on the ferocity of his motley army, but the rest were just piddling poodles alongside this two-gun mastiff.

'Mebbe,' he grunted. 'All right, *compañeros*, let's hustle. First streak of dawn, we're on our way. Tomorrow we fight again for the South and the Cause.' His voice rose to a shout. 'What do we fight for, Mechanics?'

'The South and the Cause!'

The roar from half a hundred throats shook the spruces and trembled the waters of the paternoster lakes. The Mechanics were eager for battle. They had no knowledge of a place called Creation Basin, later to be renamed Rockies Boothill.

TEN

GUNSMOKE REDEMPTION

The wind stung his gritty eyes as he stared over the graceful dish of the valley. Just the sight of the cabin squatting solid and secure in the afternoon light eased some of the weight he carried inside, which he must carry forever now.

Seemed everything here looked just as he left it.

He glanced back. The trail that had led him off to his dark destiny had brought him safely back. Ransom's set features betrayed nothing of what he was thinking in that telling moment. Perhaps he reflected on the dead: on Buck Conway who had likely deserved to die, and Marshal Bourke who had come perilously close. But more than likely, with the cabin in his sights, and watching that reassuring haze of woodsmoke drift lazily from the fieldstone chimney, he was thinking only that the tempest of violence that had overtaken him on the plains appeared to have had no bloody echo back here.

Whatever the case, he sat his saddle motionless by an ancient basalt boulder for long minutes until he caught the glint of light flashing on something metallic over there – Duval's telescope was his guess. He moved the played-out horse forward with a light pressure of the knees and steeled himself for what lay ahead for himself, and for what he must tell them. Not everything, of course; not about the marshal or the exact circumstances under which her husband had died. But what he must relate to Laura Conway had to be about as bad as news could get.

Turned out their news took precedence over his own, and it was a cruel hit to the heart for Jack Ransom to learn that Link Cassidy was dead, gunned down at Glacier Canyon. Hush was apologetic and stricken with guilt, but Ransom had no recriminations. Men did what they felt they must, was his only reaction. He was living proof of that.

'The Lord giveth and the Lord taketh away,' intoned the burning-eyed stranger with the wind-tossed mane and sonorous voice. 'Take off your hat, boy, and I'll give you the blessing and thank Jesus on your behalf for bringing you back safe to your friends and admirers, yessuh. Allelulia!'

Duval belatedly introduced Ramblin' Brother John, whom Ransom fixed with a suspicious look.

'I don't need any welcome from you or your God, mister,' he said roughly. 'Seems neither of

132

you are ever anyplace to be found when a man could use some real help.'

Thinking of what had happened. Angry. Seeking an outlet for his guilt.

'Hah! A prideful one if I'm not mistaken,' Brother John declared with some relish. 'Met a thousand of your breed, sonny, and never met one that wasn't eventually brought low by that fearsome sin of pride. . . .'

Ransom shoved the man roughly aside. He was that strung out, that contemptuous.

'Hey, easy, Ransom,' Duval intervened. 'Brother John is the genuine article, none of your bogus Bible-basher about him.'

He went on to offer a brief but flattering testimonial of the red-faced pastor, emphasizing how he'd helped them survive his absence simply by the power of his presence.

'Pride, pride, pride,' Brother John muttered in the background until Hush silenced him with a warning look.

Ransom then eased up some and concentrated as the others switched the focus of the discussion to apprise him of the Mechanics and what was known or guessed about the gang's presence out below Ghost Mountain. Naturally he'd heard the outlaws mentioned often in Plainsville in relation to Conway and the Stageville killings. He'd been little interested then but began to pay attention as he realized firstly that the big gang was fact and not fiction after all and, secondly and far more vitally, that they were camped within fifteen miles of where he now stood and 'loaded for bear' as Ramblin' Brother John predicted they would have to be as a result of the Hush–Cassidy invasion of their patch.

Sure, Ransom was intensely interested. But where was she?

It was as if he'd posited his question telepathically, for Laura suddenly appeared in the porch doorway with one hand white against her apron, the other brushing back a clump of dark hair.

He swallowed hard and knew instantly that it had all been worthwhile. The way he'd turned his back on a lifetime of morality and fair play; his cold and deliberate setting up of a bad man for the kill. Aging years in forty-eight hours in the process and acquiring a chill in the blood he might never shuck off. But worth every bit of it, or so her appearance reassured him.

He went to her, motioning the others back as they made to follow. Removing his hat, he mounted the porch steps and took her extended hand.

'Laura.' His voice was soft. He squeezed her fingers, then experienced a jolt of shock as he stared into her eyes. She already knew about Conway, he saw. If he was wrong about that then he'd never been right in his life.

He ushered her inside to deliver the bad news away from curious eyes and ears. Yet Laura showed little reaction as he described how Conway had been shot to death attempting to escape custody at Plainsville Courthouse. Ransom stood, slowly massaging the back of his neck, half-relieved and half-confounded by her stoic calm as she moved away from him to set the coffee on the pot-belly.

She must have sensed his puzzlement.

'I feared I might never see Buckley alive the day Harry and I quit the plains,' she explained. 'There was already an aura of death about him. I could feel it. I believe I knew him better than anyone, and my intuition warned me he was rushing head-long towards death from the moment he murdered those two men at our home.'

'Murdered, you say?'

'Of course.' At last Laura showed some real emotion as she lowered herself to a three-legged stool, hands twisted together in her lap. 'I'll never forget that night. We were upstairs when the outlaws entered our yard. Buck knew the Mechanics were after him, but they didn't know we were at home. We were hidden up on the balcony. Suddenly he drew his gun, and I screamed. But it was too late. He shot them down from behind like animals.' She looked up. 'My husband was a cold-blooded killer, Jack. As well as a twister, con man or crook, call him what you will. He was all those things and more . . . he was my husband.'

His heart leapt. It was strengthening to hear her denigrate Conway this way. It boosted his hopes. And yet he was even more confused.

'Yet you were still willing to kill yourself rather than testify against him? A low killer? It doesn't seem to make sense.'

She rose with a hint of impatience.

'He was my husband. Of course I was horrified by what he'd done. But I wouldn't compound the evil by sending him to the gallows. That would be a sin.'

He wanted to touch her again, but didn't.

'You understand of course that you're free now? Hear what I'm saying, girl? Conway's dead and you can live.'

Hoping desperately that this was the real reason he'd engineered the killer's end. The noble reason. To save Laura.

'You . . . you almost sound as if you hated him, Laura.'

At last came the tears.

'No. Hate is also a sin. But I no longer loved Buck. I did once, of course. But that died even before the shootings. He got drunk one night and admitted he'd only married me in order to get a solid roof over his head and some collateral behind him.' She almost whispered. 'He fell in love with my dowry, not me.'

He didn't catch all she said after this due to the pounding in his head. But he'd certainly heard her declare she had not loved Buck Conway. It was all he'd wanted to hear, his reward for what he'd done; the terrible thing he'd done. He moved to take her in his arms, but halted as boots clattered on the porchboards. Moments later a pale and breathless Harry Duval rushed in to warn of an approaching dust cloud rising steeply over Squaw Trail from the west.

*

Through the polished lens of the sea captain's brass telescope, the distant moving dots slowly emerged first as blobs then became indistinct shapes and finally resolved into the unmistakable outline of riders on horseback. A swarm of riders, the sunset haze winking menacingly from gunmetal and harness fittings, heading their way.

Harry Duval lowered his glass with a ragged sigh and drew a hand across a clammy brow. He was once again seated astride the lodgepole of the cabin like a rider who hoped his four-walled steed might suddenly rise from the earth and take flight to carry him away to safety, like a cumbersome Pegasus.

Duval was no hero and never pretended to be one. It might well be reassuring to look down and see three men at least acting out that role in the yard, but what he'd just seen out there chilled him to the bone and it was going to take more than the bravado of others to convince him they were not all going to die.

'Armed to the teeth and ugly as sin!' he called down hoarsely. 'It can only be the Mechanics. And looks like you calculated right, Hush. Better than forty riders strong, I make it. And that ain't all of it, neither.'

'What's the rest?' demanded Ransom from the barn where he was busy saddling the horses for their impending flight.

'They've got a remuda of maybe sixty loose horses driving behind them.' He paused as all three froze and stared up at him. 'And they are surely headed this way.'

Deliberately, Ransom rested the rifle he'd been carrying against the barn wall. Word of the remuda hit him like a body-blow, just as it did the others. A relief horse-herd meant there was no way the outlaws could be outrun. The dark was coming down but that would be of little help. Even if they were to flee, immediately the Mechanics, using up their fresh mounts in relays, would surely gather them in within a couple of hours, maybe even sooner.

A muffled pulsebeat seemed to throb beneath the unnatural quiet that descended.

It was Brother John who finally spoke up.

'In which case,' he said briskly, as though half-way through a sermon, 'we shall just have to stand and fight. In the Saviour's name, of course.'

Everyone began talking at once. The preacher-man attempted to silence them with upraised hands and a fierce glare, but Ransom refused to acknowledge his brand of authority.

'What would you know about fighting, you holy fraud?' he challenged contemptuously.

'I've been fighting in the front line for the Lord all my life,' came the bragging response, 'and lived to tell the tale. But should we pitch ourselves against the might of this arm of Satan's army, I know that all of us here will surely be shaking hands with the Creator by darkdown.'

He drew up and puffed out his chest.

'But I am as familiar with Satan's works as with my holy Saviour's. I know how his minions think, how to reason with them. That's my sort of fighting, brethren. With words and sweet reason I now intend to go to parley with these hellions and attempt to secure our lives. That's the sort of fighting I know about, Brother Ransom. And I shall prevail. People trust me, even sinners. So don't try to stop me.'

Nobody did. Even Ransom seemed dazed by the turn of events, by the desperate situation they now found themselves in. Laura eventually found her voice and called after Brother John as he briskly strode off into the deepening gloom. But he simply waved back and kept on, leaving barn and horse yard quickly behind, an improbably heroic figure insinuated into a chilling situation. Almost the Clown playing Hamlet. But this was no play. This was as real as it ever got.

'Well, I guess our worries are over,' Dusty Hush said mockingly. 'We can leave it all to Holybones.'

None responded. In the unnatural stillness everyone was staring across at Ransom, instinctively looking to him for leadership. But he was unaware, gripped by the bitter irony of finding himself facing yet another potentially murderous situation after all the hell he'd been through. When all he'd craved was peace, flight with the woman he loved, the chance to put Plainsville, the guilt and the violence behind him. Was that asking so much?

He shook his head and forced himself to focus on the here and now. Squaring his shoulders and double checking his guns, he drifted back towards the horse yard to stare westward.

Should he jump astride Blue and go haul Brother John back before the fool got himself killed? Or was it even remotely possible that the sinbuster might come up with a miracle by way of a bloodless solution to their plight?

He clenched his jaws and rested elbows on the teeth-gnawed top rail of the yard fence. He knew that deep down he didn't honestly believe the preacher could achieve anything with that dog pack, which meant the Mechanics would attack. The abyss yawned.

He didn't realize Laura had rejoined them until she called in that even voice from the porch.

'I'm making johnny cakes. Come on inside, everybody. We must keep up our strength.'

Her calmness reached them all. Ransom was filled with pride in her . . . then remembered what the Rambler had said about the virtue or vice of pride.

Duval and Hush vanished indoors, by so doing demonstrating implicit confidence in Rambling John's mission of madness. A short time later Ransom found himself following the others into the cabin. But he wasn't holding out any hope, couldn't eat if they paid him. Pessimism gripped him. Whatever time he had left he wanted to spend with the woman he loved.

After Hush and Duval drifted outside again, Ransom and Laura remained quietly indoors together a long time, although he seemed to have little awareness of time passing. He didn't emerge again until they heard Harry shouting from the roof that Brother John was returning by the light of a rising moon.

Ransom was impressed. He had to be. The preacher was totally unscathed, a little dejected perhaps, but plainly unharmed. By this time they had no need of Duval's telescope to see the enemy. The outlaws were now clearly visible to the naked eye, drawn up in dusty ranks out by the white pine and granite sector of Squaw Trail where Ransom had fought it out with the Smiths. So many of them! Cruel and menacing shapes etched sharply against an innocent sky.

'Well?' Jack demanded of the preacherman.

Brother John talked fast, as usual. As anticipated, he'd found himself already well known to several amongst Pickett's scum army. This had guaranteed him at least a hearing from the leader, whom he'd found curiously distracted. He'd subsequently discovered that the band did indeed intend attacking the cabin in reprisal for the two Mechanics slain and the several others wounded in the clash in the canyon. The two Southerners killed had been saddle pards of Pickett's deadliest lieutenant. So Dusty Hush, identified by the Smiths, must die, Pickett had declared. It followed that all in the valley would perish; this was his logic. Having revealed their murderous intent, Pickett had then magnanimously invited Brother John to stand by while they did what they'd come to do, after which he could preside over the buryings.

There had been no overt threat to Brother John

at any time. Wandering preachers were icons of the Deep South experience. Besides, Pickett seemed perplexingly pleased to parley with an emissary from the cabin for reasons Brother John was eventually made aware of in a private session with the gang boss.

The Mechanics had had all scouts deployed to the east for several days in preparation for their march to the plains. As a consequence, sightings had been made of a plains posse drawing worryingly close across Skyline Plateau. Obsessed with getting the jump on the possemen, Pickett had no real interest in Eliza Valley, he stated candidly, and quickly revealed a ready interest in cutting a deal with Brother John and overriding the protests both of his henchman and the Smith clan.

Pickett was prepared to settle just for Hush, and advised that if John delivered up the Mechanic-killer to satisfy their honor he would be prepared to leave the valley dwellers unharmed and the army would continue on its way south without delay.

'Would you describe this as a genuine proposition for our consideration?' the preacher now asked, with an ironic lift of bushy brows. 'Or is it an insult to a man of integrity such as yourself, Brother Ransom? How do you interpret it, my son?'

A twisted smile worked Ransom's pale face. He realized he was being offered his life and Laura's on a platter. Yet the enemy might have offered him all Wyoming Territory and his answer would still have to be the same. No deal. He had already compromised his honor in a way he'd never dreamed possible. But no further. Not one inch further.

'Take up your positions,' was the quiet way he announced his decision. And gazing across at the woman, thought: maybe it's better this way. Had they survived, he'd planned to flee West with her and lose themselves in some Pacific hideaway where he felt confident they could escape the law, if not the truth. Not forever, they couldn't. Sooner or later the true story of what had happened on the plains would seep through, and she would hate him. Wasn't it better to die with her esteem intact? He nodded yes – hoping he believed it. 'Laura, you stay indoors loading the guns. Do you use a gun, Padre?'

Both Brother John and Dusty Hush were beaming as though his decision to embrace death was the one they'd hoped he would make.

'I am armed with the Word, which shall prevail against all mine enemies,' the Rambler stated. He glanced towards the trail, where there seemed to be some kind of disturbance taking place amongst the enemy now. 'I estimate we might have roughly one half-hour to live, an hour at the most. So, who shall be first to make his peace with his Maker?'

Ransom experienced a jolt of unreality as his companions immediately indicated interest in this bizarre offer. He could understand Laura seeking absolution, he supposed, her being so devout. But the notion of a hellraiser like Dusty Hush looking to cleanse his well-grimed soul instead of spending what time he had left readying his guns and ammunition struck him as almost ludicrous.

Yet that passage of time during which the other three, in turn, visited with the preacherman indoors, while he slowly paced the perimeter with Winchester and Colts, had a profound effect on the mountain man with blood on his hands. He'd already reconciled to the fact that he must die here. But the hardest aspect to come to terms with was not that he would be denied his time with Laura Conway, but rather the oppressive awareness of his crime.

Maybe he could use some final words of hope for the hereafter after all. . . .

Seated in an old chair by the kitchen window, the preacher seemed unsurprised when the tall figure came in to lean a shoulder against a roof support, staring down at him.

'Kneel, son,' he said gently.

'Why should I?'

Brother John leaned back and folded his arms. 'Prideful to the last, eh? Pride won't get you into Paradise, Ransom.'

'I killed a man,' he blurted out abruptly.

'Huh?'

'I murdered Laura's husband. And I shot Marshal Bourke.'

Brother John rose slowly to his feet. 'But this can't be so, son. I know of your reputation. You are a man of character and integrity. I've seen this and felt it myself—'

144

Ransom cut him off with a torrent of words, spilling out a naked and ungarnished account of everything that had happened. He even admitted to his motive, his all-consuming motive. He'd fallen in love for the first time and had been driven to do things in its name such as he could never have done before. It was as though he'd been in the grip of something stronger than himself, he tried to explain, knowing the while that nothing could explain or justify what had been done.

Yet as soon as he unburdened himself of his awful secret, there was an immediate easing of the pain. But not of the guilt. He was looking to the preacher for that.

'You're suffering, son. . .'

'Yeah.'

'And so you should, so you should. For it is surely a terrible thing you've done. And to a top-lofty and stiff-necked *hombre* such as yourself, it must be doubly hard to know you are as weak and base as the lowliest man alive. But take heart, Ransom, we are all capable of any evil. You, me, all of us are the sons of Cain: vile, violent and murderous at heart. It's in the Book. But there is always redemption while ever there is life. So kneel and I will bless you . . .'

Brother John broke off as voices rose sharply beyond the window, where Dusty Hush's shaggy head suddenly appeared.

'Jack!' the man shouted excitedly. 'The main bunch is movin' off, but there's a squad of riders a-comin' our way across the meadow.'

With a puzzled scowl, Ransom strode out into the flooding moonlight.

'By the eternal,' Judson Smith mouthed as the buckskinned figure appeared by the barn, 'that is him. It's Ransom. I tipped we'd find the big bastard still skulkin' here, didn't I?'

'You sure did, Daddy,' his elder son said thickly, through a broken jaw. 'But are you still sure it was a good notion for us to come in with Monk, even so?'

Monk rode a horse-length ahead. The killer's decision to launch his own private assault on the cabin had come mere minutes earlier, following the arrival of a scout from the plateau bringing the news that Needham's possemen were heading their way. Fired by the prospect of ambushing the inferior law force, Pickett lost what little interest he might have had in the valley attack and immediately announced his intention to lead the army south. Yet much as he wanted Monk by his side, he dare not refuse the gunhawk permission to break off and go seek his personal vengeance for fear of risking a confrontation.

Judson Smith, every inch as hard a hater as the breed, had insisted they join Monk in the hope of discovering the hated Ransom still here in the valley with his sidekick, Hush. Pickett, his sights fixed on something infinitely bigger, had dismissed the four with a perfunctory gesture and galloped away at the head of his column with blood in his eye, rushing unwittingly towards ambush and death on Skyline Plateau.

With one bitter son still nursing a crippled arm and the other a deformed face, the Smiths were dripping hate and radiated murderous eagerness as they now loped across the wide meadows. Even so, the trio kept glancing across for reassurance at the sombreroed Monk, a skull-faced eminence with shoulder-length hair and twin guns, by far the most menacing Mechanic of them all. Unaware of their attention, Monk only had eyes for the enemy, trying to identify Dusty Hush from the crackers' description of the man he must destroy.

However, his bleak stare quickly focused on the commanding figure in the buckskin jacket who suddenly quit the cabin yard to come striding out towards them.

What the hell was this one doing?

'That's our curly wolf, Monk,' Daddy Smith exulted. Then he frowned uncertainly. 'But what does thet stinkin' Yankee gun dog think he's a-doin'. . . ?'

'Jack, what the hell are you doing?' Dusty Hush shouted, unwittingly echoing Smith's own puzzlement as Ransom's long stride carried him beyond the barn. 'You gone loco, man?'

No response.

'Jack, please!' Laura's cry from the window caused Ransom to half-turn his head. But he kept on with the rifle in his hands and twin guns buckled around his hips as the horsemen loomed larger through the tall grass.

He was not surprised to identify the Smiths. In

truth the prospect of facing these scum yet again fired him up. He'd bested them once and might do so again, depending on the fourth man.

This one's brand was all too easy to read. Pure killer. He knew the breed on sight. The fourth man could make all the difference, he realized. But there could be no turning back now, not even had there been a dozen butchers riding with the Smiths. Nothing could halt him now. For the preacher's words still rang in his ears. 'We are all of us sons of Cain!' In so saying, Brother John had understood his sin, yet he had not absolved him of it. Ransom did not believe any preacher could do this, nor any mortal man. Yet the moment he'd glimpsed the outlaws heading for the cabin he'd sensed what this desperate situation might really be.

His chance for redemption.

Abruptly he halted and flung away his heavy rifle. It disappeared into the grass. Immediately the riders reined in, puzzled, suspecting a trick.

It was only moments before Monk's skull features twisted in an almost admiring grimace of understanding.

'Why, this bastard's got balls enough, I declare. . .'

'What? What do you mean?' puzzled Daddy Smith.

'Can't you see? He's challengin' us to a gun duel. One agin' four, by the rules. He's loco and he's gonna die, but he's got grit. . . .' The brief glint of admiration flickered from the killer's eyes. 'And you can bet a man with that kind of sand in his craw would've been at the canyon with his buddies . . . butcherin' good men. . . .' He gestured violently. 'All right, ditch the rifles, get down and follow me in.'

'W-what?' the youngest Smith almost bleated. 'Why for, man? We all don't have to play Ransom's game. We're callin' the shots. . . .'

'He's a pro,' Monk panted, jumping down and hitching at crossed gunbelts. 'He knows a man afoot's got an edge agin' riders in close-quarter stuff like this. Hosses are too big a target to miss, they can take fright. But don't wet your pants, cousins. He's mine anyways on account I'm smellin' my pards' blood all over this tall mucker now, clear and strong. He's meat!'

He started forwards, leaving the Smiths isolated and feeling suddenly vulnerable. But at a sharp word from the father, the three dismounted and hurried after the gunman's husky shape.

Ransom stood waiting, hands hanging at his sides. The clansmen fanned out instinctively as they closed in. But the Smiths might have been invisible for all the attention he paid them. The sombrero leading them in was the man. Only a supremely confident killer would respond so boldly to the kind of challenge Ransom was throwing down.

Took one to know one . . . maybe. . . .

Monk's shoulders suddenly dipped and twin guns filled his hands with astonishing speed.

'For my pards, you Yankee scumdog!' he roared, and was already triggering as Ransom came clear.

But he was way too fast. With bullets whipping wildly by him, Ransom made the double draw of his life and shot straight. The first bullet struck Monk squarely in the chest, driving him back on to his heels. Before the look of bewilderment faded from the swarthy face, Ransom killed him with a bullet through the throat which severed his wind-pipe and shattered his backbone.

Shocked and desperate, the Smiths jerked up their guns and starting in shooting.

Ransom was creased as he dived full length but was in no way hindered.

He blasted upwards from the grass at Judson Smith, who'd turned the color of parchment when Monk toppled to his doom. He caught the man with one slug that smashed his knee, then a second that punched in just beneath the jaw then contin-ued upwards through the top of the skull to splat-ter his eldest son in crimson.

Next instant saw the terrified Smith sons in full retreat. They rushed back to their mounts to go heeling away, crouched low over their horses' necks as they careened back the way they'd come in blind terror, steel-shod hoofs flipping dark clods high in their wake.

Ransom did not shoot again. There was no need.

Emotion twisted his face as he sat up in the grass massaging a bullet-creased leg. He felt triumphant, but that was a long way short of feeling redeemed.

There it was again.

The dark riders crossing the basin behind Pickett saw the man twist suddenly in his saddle for the third time in as many minutes, as though either confused or jittery.

They didn't figure. The mob was making good time and there was nothing about Creation Basin to cause concern. The walls were a safe half-mile distant on either side of the column, the moon was bright and there wasn't enough cover anyplace to hide a decent-sized gnat.

So why was the most dangerous man in the mountains acting as nervous as the Bride of Montezuma on her wedding night?

There were two reasons, but Pickett was keeping both to himself. The first was Monk's absence. Pickett relied on the lethal gunman more than anyone realized, and there was still no sign of his backtrail. The other cause of his cold-sweat jitters was the basin itself. He'd not felt right ever since they started across, although why this should be so he had no inkling. Wide open and featureless, it looked about the safest stretch of real estate in the high country. Yet if that was the case, why wouldn't his neck hair settle?

It might have been a psychic awareness that, not one hundred yards distant, the silver gunsights of an invisible .45-70 Springfield rifle had just locked in on the side of his head an inch below the brim of his turned-down hat.

The Springfield was rock steady in the brawny hands of Marshal Needham whose tall strong body ached savagely from two hours cramped up in a body hole designed to accommodate a Shoshone warrior half his size.

There were forty such pits in the featureless face of the basin floor, all but six occupied by a posse-man with a gun. They'd taken up their positions hours earlier and a scout had covered each rifle-man with his groundsheet which was then coated in a layer of dust rendering it virtually invisible on either side of the track the prudent killers were taking down the center of the basin.

It was in Needham simply to open up, but he was too much the by-the-book peace officer for that.

'This is Marshal Needham!' he roared in a bull-horn voice. 'And I'm calling on you to surrender and—'

He got no further. The outlaw column exploded into instant desperate action, raking with spurs, filling their hands with guns in an instant of fatal panic.

Needham's first shot blew Pickett out of his saddle where he lay bleeding and dying with his face to the moon, unable to move yet conscious of everything going on about him. He saw men and horses going down in a welter of dust and gushing crimson all about him, heard, ragged and shrill through the snarl of the ambush rifles, the death scream of his first lieutenant as he nosedived into the earth with his broad brimmed hat rolling free like a cartwheel.

His brave Mechanics were being riddled from either side of the murderous trail. His dream was bleeding into the dust of Creation Basin, and he could not believe any of it. He tried to roar out his anathema and rage but he choked on blood.

Jack Ransom was puzzled when Laura did not seem to understand what he was leading up to as they stood together in the kitchen window watching Duval harnessing the horse to the trap outside. She appeared unaware that these would be the most fateful moments they would ever share. In the brief silence between them could be heard the distant mutter of a gun battle far to the south, the outcome of which no longer had any bearing on Eliza Valley. It didn't exist for him. Nothing did but making her understand.

'But, Laura, don't you see? We'll all go together, you, Harry, Dusty and me. You've got to leave in case Needham survives that dust-up then comes looking for you. As for me, well, I'm all through with the mountains anyway. The West is ours, yours and mine. Don't you understand? We're free.'

'No, I don't think I do understand, Jack,' she answered, plainly perplexed. 'I have to get away, certainly. But Harry and I are headed for Oregon. Why on earth would you want to go there?'

'To be with you, of course.'

Laura's brow furrowed. 'With me?'

He took her by the shoulders. She was the loveliest thing he'd ever seen.

'With you. Forever. Can't you see it, Laura? Haven't you known all along. I'm in love with you.'

'Oh . . . oh, Jack, I'm so sorry.'

'Sorry?' He let his hands drop. 'Sorry for what?'

'Dearest Jack, I'll be grateful all my life for what you've done here for us. You'll always be close to my heart. But I don't love you . . . and I had no notion you felt that way about me.'

He reeled back as though struck. He couldn't believe it. Yet her calm, grave look gave him no option. It had never once occurred to him that should the great Jack Ransom ever set pride and vanity aside long enough to fall in love, this might not guarantee the happy ending he'd always secretly craved.

His look of naked agony demanded something more, and characteristically Laura Conway did not disappoint him.

He would never forget the way she looked as she spoke softly to him, explaining how it was with her. She had fallen in love just once in her life, and that proved a terrible mistake. Now she was going to Oregon to settle with a Quaker colony she knew of there, somewhere where she would be safe even from an obsessive Needham, where she could forget the past. If she had given Ransom cause to think her affection and respect for him could be something more, he must forgive her. Would he?

But he could not speak. Half-way to heaven? Or was it hell?

'Goodbye, dearest Jack. I'll never forget you.'

He didn't recall walking outside to find himself face to face with Ramblin' Brother John. The preacherman was rigged up for the trail. He planned to accompany Laura and Duval all the way to Oregon to do some 'Far West-style sinbusting', as he termed it.

The man studied Ransom sagaciously as though he understood everything.

'It would never have worked, son.'

'What . . . what are you talking about?'

'She doesn't know the true story yet but she will in time. The truth is like that. You allowed her husband to be slain, and you shot up a good man. There is no way you could either deny or answer that. So in the end she'd despise you and it would have failed anyway. But will you fail, Brother Jack? Who knows? After risking your life to save all of ours, Lord Jesus may well forgive you even if man and the law do not. You sinned as did Cain, boy, but you were surely Abel, the hero and good son in this place. So who can say?' He paused, and almost whispered, 'So, whither thou goest now, my son?'

Ransom had no answer to that. The preacher raised his hand in a blessing and was gone, striding across to the waiting trap to clamber up behind the couple perched upon the high seat. Moments later the rig rolled from the yard with Laura and Duval waving back at the solitary figure before the cabin, with Brother John standing in back with both arms stretched wide as though to embrace all the mighty West.

'Goddamn, how'd you manage that, *amigo*?' an impressed and innocent Dusty Hush chuckled, leading the saddle horses from the barn across to the porch. 'Get shook of 'em, I mean? I figgered that clingin' little widder would sink her hooks

155

into you so deep you'd never bust loose. I reckoned you'd need a pardon from the governor to shake her off. But you've come out ahead and whistle-clean again. Packed her off neat as you like, and the old team lives to fight another day.'

He halted the horses and punched Ransom's shoulder, grinning admiringly. Big simple Dusty was unaware of the truth or the reality. Ransom would reveal it all in time, maybe. But not yet. Not now.

He wordlessly drew a flask from the patch-pocket of his buckskin jacket and slowly unscrewed the cap. The trap had almost disappeared from sight.

Hush remained unconscious of his mood as he clapped him on the back.

'Too bad old Link ain't here to see all this, Jack. But of course he wouldn't be surprised to see how things have turned out for you. He'd be first to agree that the nickname we give you all that time back never fitted better than today, huh?'

Jack Ransom was staring bleakly into the empty years ahead as he lifted the flask to his lips. He was a hollow man, an empty shell. The life ahead lay bleak and stark before him. He'd never dare return to the Rockies. He would change his name, maybe take up a few remote acres in the California wilderness, live in hope that not even a bloodhound such as Needham would or could hunt him that far. Live quiet, never attract attention, trust no man.

The new life and times of a 'hero'.

But there was one desperately small thing to cling to, even so. For Laura would always be with him. He had fallen in love with her, thereby allaying the only real fear he'd ever known – namely that he could not love as other men did. And what he'd done once he might do again. If he survived, if the Preacher's God ever forgave him, if there was another Laura out there.

One slim hope, Ransom. Slim as a sliver. But it was all he had so it had to be enough.

'That's me right enough, Dusty,' he agreed drily as they swung up. 'Jack the Winner all the way.'